THE INSIDE MAN

A CORPS JUSTICE NOVEL

C. G. COOPER

"THE INSIDE MAN"

Warning: This story is intended for mature audiences and contains profanity and violence.

FOUR FREE BOOKS!

Download the ultimate C. G. Cooper Starter Kit:
FOUR FREE NOVELS!
Visit cg-cooper.com to download. No email required.

PROLOGUE

NEW YORK CITY

"Pulitzer Prize Winning Prick," Logan Whitaker murmured as he resisted the urge to slam the glass door. He turned and waved at the writer who'd assigned him a last-minute source check. Stupid newspaper rules.

"And I want it in person. You got that? I need it pronto."

In person. After work. This wasn't what Logan thought his life would be like. Studying journalism at Stanford, the talented writer dreamed of digging up political dirt and claiming his own Pulitzer.

That dream shattered on Day One when his real boss, the managing editor for *The Continental Ledger*, instructed him to do anything and everything that this award-winning lead writer needed. Yes, that included fetching coffee, getting his shoes shined, and making dinner reservations.

Six months and a two pairs of Johnston & Murphy dress shoes later, Logan didn't think he could make it another day.

"Screw it," he said. His finger stabbed the elevator button over and over again until it opened. He was supposed to be on a date. He'd had to cancel again. No way she'd go out with him now. Nice girl. Gorgeous eyes. He imagined what it would be like to wake up next to her, as the elevator drifted down floors.

The elevator dinged, and he slouched into the lobby, grimacing when he pushed out into the city. Stiff wind whipped down the street. He hugged his coat close. A storm was coming.

That was when he realized he hadn't made the call.

Turning his back to the wintry blast, he pulled out the sheet of paper. Ten sources were on the list. The writer had circled two. There was a phone number and an address next to each name. He reached into his pocket and groaned. He'd left his phone upstairs. The last thing he wanted to do was go back up to the office.

Whitaker looked at the list again and saw that one of the circled names had an address he recognized. It was a couple of blocks from his own apartment. He'd stop by, unannounced, confirm what needed confirming, go home, use his roommate's cell phone, and finish his duties for the night. Hopefully.

Whitaker shielded himself as best he could as he walked. He wasn't used to city winters. *I need to buy a warmer coat,* he thought.

Logan looked up at the building. He'd already tried the buzzer. No one answered.

"Great. Another night wasted."

He tried to shove his hands even deeper into his pockets. Maybe the best play was to go home, get a better coat, or three, make the phone calls, and confirm the facts for the story. How would the writer know he hadn't gotten the confirmation in person? It was a stupid story. A complete waste of time. At least that's what Logan thought.

But a stint at *The Continental Ledger* meant something. Once a beacon of global journalism, the old paper almost drowned over three decades of poor management and a stubborn connection to the past. Now, with new ownership, the paper was on the rise, thanks to a knack for finding timely hits before the competition.

That's why Logan waited outside the building, thinking. That's why he had the hunch that the man hurrying up the street was the very man he was here to see.

"Mr. Petersen?"

The man looked up. Logan noticed the scruffy beard, leery eyes.

"Who's asking?"

"Logan Whitaker, with *The Continental Ledger.*"

The man made a shooing gesture that Logan was immune to. He'd learned to press.

"Mr. Petersen, I'm here to confirm the—"

"Look, pal, I'm busy, okay? And why the hell didn't you call first?"

Logan wasn't about to tell him the real reason.

"Sir, this is an important story, one that could—"

Niles Petersen stopped and glared at Logan. He tried to look tough. But Logan was bigger, younger, and much stronger. Petersen's gaze shifted. Logan knew he had him.

"No," Petersen said, his eyes looking over Logan's shoulder. The source started backing away, and Logan turned. The smell hit him first. Stale body odor and swill liquor. The newcomer's face was filthy, and he grinned with yellow teeth.

Logan backed away, too. And that's when he noticed it. Everything fit except for the homeless man's eyes. They were clear and zeroed in on Petersen. A few stutter steps and the man fell upon Petersen. His hand jerked forward and back, over and over.

He's got a knife, Logan realized. *He's stabbing him.*

It was over quickly. The man never looked at Logan, just let Petersen slip to the ground, then stumbled away.

Logan finally unglued his feet and rushed to help Petersen. The source was actually smiling.

"I should've known," Petersen said, his voice in wonder.

Logan put a hand to the man's chest. He pulled it away, realizing the man was gushing blood. He replaced his hand and cried out, "Help!"

Petersen was saying something.

Logan cursed himself for not having a phone. He wasn't about to root through the dying man's pocket to see if he had one.

"It's okay. You're gonna be okay," Logan said, because he thought that's what he was supposed to say.

Petersen was still talking to himself.

"What?" Logan asked, though he was more concerned with finding someone, anyone, who could take his spot.

Why's the street so empty? Can't anyone hear me?

"Help!" he called out again.

Nothing.

Petersen grabbed Logan's arm.

Logan didn't want to look, but he did. Even in the dim light, he could see that Petersen's face was deathly pale.

"Just like Jimmy," Petersen said.

"What? Who's Jimmy?"

Petersen laughed, convulsed, and then lie still.

I should do CPR, Logan thought. But he didn't know how to do CPR.

That's when the cop car showed up with an ambulance right behind. One cop pulled Logan to his feet while the other did CPR. The first cop pushed Logan against the cruiser and frisked him.

"What are you doing?" Logan asked.

"I was about to ask you the same thing, kid."

"I was trying to save that guy's life."

"You know him?"

"What? No."

It wasn't exactly the truth, but it wasn't a lie either.

"What happened?" the cop asked, turning Logan around.

"He got stabbed."

"By who?"

"Some homeless guy."

"You get a good look at him?" The cop glanced over at his partner, who had been joined by two paramedics.

"Not really. It's dark and—"

"You live around here?"

"A couple blocks away."

"And you say you don't know this guy?"

"No. Never met him in my life."

"And you just happened to be what? Going home?"

The lie came naturally. "Yeah."

"Late night at the office?" the cop asked. There was zero urgency in the man's tone. The paramedics hoisted Petersen's body onto a gurney.

"What?" Logan asked, tearing his eyes from the body being wheeled away.

"I said, late night at the office?"

"Um, yeah. Lots of late nights."

The cop nodded.

"Listen, kid. We need to escort the ambulance to the hospital. There's gonna be another team here soon. You stay and answer their questions, got it?"

"Yes, officer."

The cop patted him on the back with a gloved hand.

Then they were gone, not with flashing lights and sirens. Just gone.

Logan sat down on the curb and waited.

No one ever came.

CHAPTER 1

LOGAN WHITAKER

Logan Whitaker waited four hours for the police to arrive. When they didn't show, he dragged himself home, took a shower, threw away his blood-stained clothes, took a shot of tequila, and then called the police.

When he described why he was calling, he was put on a brief hold. When the person came back on the line, she said, "Are you sure you got the name right?"

"Yes. Last name is Petersen. First name Niles."

Logan heard clicking on the other end. "Sorry. We don't have any record of a Niles Petersen."

"Look, ma'am, I don't want to sound rude, but I've had a very long night. Could you please check again?"

He could hear her hesitation. But then the clacking started. Then stopped.

"I've checked every spelling I can think of, sir."

"You think I imagined it?!"

"Sir, I'm just telling you what the system is telling me. Why don't you come down to the station and we'll take your statement?"

That's when it hit Logan. Wasn't that what the cops were supposed to ask him when they came to the scene of the crime? His mind caught up.

"Um, sure. I'll, uh, be down there soon."

He ended the call and threw his roommate's phone on the couch.

"I'm not crazy," he said to the empty room.

The list. He'd forgotten about the list.

Logan went to the bathroom and found the list of sources lying on the floor next to the toilet. Dried blood crinkled one corner. He tore off the corner and flushed it down the toilet. Then he looked at the list.

Petersen, Niles. The first circled name. Logan's eyes scanned down and stopped on the fourth name: Jimmy. Petersen had said something about Jimmy. What was it? Something like, "Jimmy did it too." No, that wasn't right. Think, Logan!

It hit him.

"Just like Jimmy," he said, remembering how Petersen had said it.

What the hell was that supposed to mean? Was Petersen comparing his fate to Jimmy's? And who was Jimmy other than a name on the source list?

"This is nuts. Maybe you are going crazy." He looked at himself in the mirror. His mother would not be happy. In his pursuit to be a model journalist, he'd lost close to twenty pounds, hadn't been to the gym in three months, and wore the coloring of a man who spent his days under fluorescent lights.

He looked at the list again.

What if Petersen survived? Maybe the wounds weren't as bad as they looked.

"Yep, I'm definitely going nuts."

Logan fetched the phone from the couch, then dialed the number next to Niles Petersen's name.

You're nuts. You're nuts. You're —

"Who is this?" a man's sleepy voice answered.

"I'm sorry to bother you at this hour," Logan said, doing his best to sound professional. "but is this Niles Petersen?"

"Yes, it is. Who is this?"

At first, Logan couldn't answer.

"I said, who is this?"

Logan somehow regained his composure.

"Sir, this is Logan Whitaker from *The Continental Tribune*. I'm calling about a story we're running concerning yesterday's breakdown at the border."

The man's voice was clearer now. "Well, why didn't you lead with that?" Logan heard shuffling like the man was sitting up in bed. "You want to do this over the phone or in person?"

Logan gulped.

"In person. If that's okay."

"Sure. No problem. You have my address, I assume?"

"Yes, sir."

"Good. I'll have a pot of coffee ready when you get here."

Logan stared at the phone and somehow gathered his wits enough to say, "I'll be there in fifteen minutes."

Logan expected to find police tape and splash of crusted blood on the concrete when he arrived at the same address where he'd sat for the better part of the night. There was no blood and no police tape. A hunched woman shuffled by with her walker and Logan let her pass, still wondering if he should be here.

This is a game. It has to be, Logan thought.

When he buzzed Unit 11, Niles Petersen told him to come up.

The Niles Petersen who answered the door was not the

same Niles Petersen who'd been stabbed the night before. This Niles Petersen handed him a mug of coffee, then led him into the living room. Petersen, still in his pajamas, looked at ease and welcoming.

"You wanna record this, or…"

Logan had to shake his head to snap back to reality. He tapped his temple. "I've got an excellent memory."

"You sure? If you forgot your notepad, I can grab you some paper."

Too welcoming, was the thought that hit Logan's brain center.

"No thanks. Debate club honed my detail skills."

"I wish I had that talent." Petersen crossed one leg over the other. "You want me to start, or do you have specific questions?"

Logan was glad for the offer.

"Why don't you run it from the beginning? I'll chime in when I need clarification."

"No problem. So it all started two days ago…"

Logan listened to the man's story. It was all very professional, very convincing, and very much in line with what the paper needed. But he couldn't shake the feeling that it was all a charade, and that the man sitting across from him was a wonderful actor.

CHAPTER 2

DANIEL BRIGGS

Daniel Briggs pulled Anna Varushkin close. "I'm gonna miss you," he said.

"Then come with me. Paris is beautiful at Christmas." She leaned in and kissed him. "Besides, you owe me."

"Do I?" he said, grazing a thumb along her jawline.

"You do. You promised you'd take dancing lessons."

Daniel laughed. "*That's* what I owe you?"

"You promised."

Anna made a fake pouty face. She did not have a pouty personality. Not in the slightest.

"You'd dance circles around me," he said.

"That's the point. Something I can do better than you."

"Ah. Now I see."

She looked down at her watch. "Shoot. I have to go. Last chance. Christmas in Paris?"

"I wish I could, but I've been gone long enough."

This time she pulled him in for a long kiss, ignoring the New Yorkers who looked at them as they hurried to their trains.

"Be careful," he said. Her hand slipped from his.

She blew him a kiss and gave him a wink.

Daniel watched her go. He nodded to the two bodyguards. They blended into the crowd. No one would know they were with Anna. They were very good at their jobs. He'd made sure of that.

"Time to get to work," he said to himself. First, he wanted to read a newspaper. His time recuperating in Europe had done him good. But he missed America. His home.

The newspaper stand had a line of ten people long. Daniel stepped to the end and waited, his eyes scanning. There was a young man sitting on a bench, head in hands. The first thing Daniel thought was the man was at the tail-end of his previous night, though it was almost ten in the morning.

The line moved slowly, and Daniel's gaze kept coming back to the young man. He hadn't moved.

Daniel paid for a copy of *The Continental Tribune* with cash pocketing the change. When he turned, the guy was still on the bench.

Leave him alone, Daniel told himself.

But he couldn't. It wasn't in his nature. Especially not now. He'd been through too much. He'd been the recipient of goodwill. It was impossible for him not to help.

He walked to the bench. "Mind if I sit?" he asked.

The young man didn't look up, but he scooted over.

"Thanks," Daniel said. He took a seat. The young man didn't smell like he'd pulled an all-nighter. Maybe he'd lost all his client's money. That was New York City.

He scanned the front page for anything of interest. Every title poked at fear and outrage. Daniel opened the paper. The young man hadn't moved.

"You okay?" Daniel asked. The young man didn't answer. Daniel reached over and tapped him on the arm. "You okay?"

"I'm fine."

"Good."

"But thanks for asking."

"No problem."

Daniel didn't chide himself for asking. That was his job. It had to be. If he didn't ask, he couldn't know. Some people just didn't want to talk. Kind of like him. Something Daniel was working on.

The young man stood up suddenly and walked away.

Daniel watched him go. He didn't know why, but he couldn't help staring. Daniel knew from long experience that no matter what he did next, he and the young man would meet again soon. Daniel said a quick prayer, asking for guidance. Then he settled in to read the rest of the paper, and wait for what the universe might offer him next.

CHAPTER 3

LOGAN WHITAKER

Logan had almost jumped out of skin when the blonde pony-tailed guy sat down next to him. He'd actually counted to one hundred, starting over twice, before getting up to leave.

The train station was his brilliant idea to be somewhere public. After the interview with Niles Petersen #2, he didn't know where else to go. Home felt unsafe. The cops had already proved they couldn't help. So what did that leave?

Work. He had to go to work.

Logan tried to put on a cheery face when he greeted the security guard. The old man gave him a look as if to say, "Did you sleep in those clothes?"

Sleep. What a luxury. Logan wasn't sure he'd ever sleep again.

He'd just slipped out of the elevator and was heading to the bathroom to tidy himself up when a voice said, "You're late, Whitaker."

Logan turned. The Pulitzer Prize Winning Prick was standing in the middle of the hallway, hands on his oversized hips. "You better have what I need. I had to ask for more time."

"Yeah, I uh, let me use the bathroom and—"

"Three minutes, Whitaker. Three minutes!" The Prick said it loud enough for the entire floor to hear.

I don't need this right now, Logan thought.

He hurried to the bathroom. No wonder the guy at the station had asked him if he was okay. He looked like a cold dish of hangover. Wetting his hair, he did his best to comb it with his hands. Then, he put his mouth under the faucet and gulped down the automatic warm water. Next came the straightening of his tie and the re-tucking of his shirt. Not terrible, but not great.

His first stop was his tiny cubicle, where he picked up his cell phone from right where he'd left it. The battery was dead. *Great.*

"Whitaker!" the Prick called. Logan heard giggling coming from another cubicle. He couldn't tell which. He didn't care.

He rushed to the Prick's corner office.

"Give it to me," the writer said. He was staring at his laptop.

"I only got in touch with one source."

"I know."

"What? How—"

"I called them myself."

The writer swiveled his chair to face Logan.

"I thought they said you had talent, Whitaker. You come in here looking like you spent the night in a bar, with confirmation from only one source, and what, you expect me to thank you?"

"It won't happen again."

The Prick grinned. "You're right. It won't. Next time you step out of line, I'll have them boot your ass back to Kansas faster than you can spell Mississippi."

Retorts came to mind, but Logan bit his tongue and nodded instead.

"Now, tell me what Petersen told you. I want to make sure I got it right."

That's when it hit Logan. The Prick hadn't called anyone.

Logan ran through what Petersen #2 told him. At various points, the prick cut in and asked a question. Apparently Logan answered each question to the Prick's satisfaction because when the story was told, the writer said, "This was your last chance. Got it?"

"Got it."

"I slept in the same suit for a week when I started. Don't use your personal hygiene as an excuse not to do good work, understand?"

"Understood."

"Now get the hell out of here. I've got an article to finish."

Maybe the writer had been talented once. Yes, Logan was impressed when he read the piece that won him the Pulitzer. But the work the Prick put out now was more gotcha and needling than actual substance. It still got the writer on top news shows and editorial pieces.

For the rest of the day, Logan busied himself with the mountain of tasks piled on his desk. He'd given up thinking that at some point he'd have a clear space to work. The business of news was ongoing. It never stopped. Not unless the world stopped, and that would not happen.

Logan skipped lunch. Can after can of energy drinks sustained him. That, and a half-eaten granola bar he'd left in a drawer. His mother called twice on his office phone. He let it go to voicemail. She probably wanted to talk about her favorite topic of the year: when Logan was going to help her sift through his father's belongings.

Brian Whitaker died a week before his son was supposed to start work in New York City. They'd somehow gotten the funeral arrangements made, ceremony conducted, and the house cleared of guests in that time. Logan only had to ask for one extra day to report in for work.

When his mother called a third time, it was almost five o'clock. Logan exhaled. He didn't hate his mom. He just hated talking about his dead father, a man he held above any other.

"Hey, Mom," Logan answered.

"Honey, you sound exhausted."

That's what she always said.

"I'm fine, Mom. How are you?"

"I'm so glad you asked. This morning, as I was cleaning out your father's desk, I found…"

And so it went for the next fifteen minutes. She never stopped. Finally, when Logan realized his attention was failing, he said, "Mom, I'm still at work."

"Oh, I'm sorry, honey. I thought you were at home."

He'd told her many times that he worked well into the night. She still thought people worked an honest nine to five. He almost told her he wasn't planning on going home, not tonight. Instead, he said, "You know how things work in the Big City, Mom. Always moving."

"You sure you're taking care of yourself, Logan? Don't forget that your father had a heart attack when he was forty-five."

"I'm twenty three, Mom."

"I know. But you're all I have left."

They'd almost finished the conversation without a sad note. He loved his mother very much. He just didn't have the energy to deal with more emotion at the moment.

"I'll see you at Christmas. Okay?"

"I can't wait. I'm cooking all your favorite things. Banana bread. Prime rib. That silly little cocktail you and your father found in Jamaica."

"You don't have to do that, Mom," Logan said.

"I know. But I want to." She paused and he could imagine her crying. "I love you, honey."

"I love you too, Mom. Talk soon."

He ended the call before more emotion could filter through the phone. Logan put the phone aside and stared at the still high pile of work. At least he had that.

But his mind went back to the night before, and like any brilliant reporter, his instincts continue to dissect what had happened, what he'd seen. The empty streets. The bum with the focused eyes. The non-existent police interview. All of it. It was midnight before he'd halved the pile, and his mind focused on what he had to do next. He remembered Niles Petersen's words: Just like Jimmy.

Logan Whitaker needed to find out about Jimmy.

He pulled out the crumpled list of sources. Jimmy Mason. It could be a coincidence. Or it could be something real. Logan had to find out which, or else he might need to get his head checked next.

CHAPTER 4

DANIEL BRIGGS

Daniel looked up at the greying sky as the first flakes of snow drifted onto the city. He was avoiding the phone call. What better way to kill time than to wander the Big Apple?

The dusting turned to gusts. Daniel slipped into a side street, meaning to cut time off his commute. He'd waited long enough. His friends needed to know that he was back in the States. It was time to get back to work.

A door banged open and a man with a dirty apron hoisted a trashcan into the street. Daniel moved aside, noting the smell of fresh bread and meatballs wafting from the restaurant's door.

The man with the trash can made a racket thumping the can all the way to the dumpster. Daniel walked past, picking up the pace.

Trashcan and worker thumped their way back to the restaurant, the door slamming shut. That's when Daniel's senses perked and made him turn, and he looked up at the emergency escape ladder.

A smile beamed down at him, matched by casually swinging legs.

"Wilcox," Daniel said, stopping to look up at the man.

"I heard you were back."

"From whom?"

"Whom? I see the Europeans rubbed off on you. Tell me, do you drink your tea with your pinky at full stretch?"

Matthew Wilcox, the wily assassin who had once kidnapped Cal Stokes, and now appeared whenever and wherever he chose, slipped from his perch and landed lightly on the pavement.

"I saw you six blocks back," Daniel said. "You were standing next to a woman with a pink scarf. You were reading a comic book. Or was it Manga?"

Wilcox clapped his gloved hands. "Very good. I see you haven't lost your touch. You all better now?"

Wilcox was referring to Daniel's own kidnapping at the hands of two old Marines who wanted a pound and a half of Daniel's flesh, and more.

"I'm fine."

"And Anna?"

"She's fine too," Daniel said.

"That's good. I like her. I'm glad you finally let your guard down enough to say yes to the dress."

Wilcox had a way with words.

"I'm busy," Daniel said.

"I can see that. You've been to two AA meetings since dropping Anna at the station. You've walked approximately eight miles. You've stopped once for a coffee and once for a snack." Wilcox scratched his head. "Now, I'm no genius, but it seems like you're avoiding something. Could it be that you and Cal are on the outs? Please tell me that ain't so. We were just figuring things out."

"Cal and I are fine."

It annoyed Daniel that Wilcox was so astute. Of course, he

and Cal were fine. How could they not be? They hadn't seen one another in months. That's what recuperative leave was: time away.

"Fabulous. So you're going to see him now? He's all the way in Virginia, you know. You don't have a car and I haven't seen an airline ticket. Train?"

What didn't Wilcox know?

"Seems like you've got too much time on your hands, Wilcox. Bored?" Daniel started walking. Wilcox followed.

"I'm always bored. If I'm not killing communists, dictators, lousy Hollywood actors or heathens, I don't know what to do with myself. I'm sure you understand how that feels."

"Not anymore," Daniel said. They hit a principal street and crossed between honking cars.

"Oh? Have you overcome our weakness?"

"What weakness is that?"

"Don't be coy, Daniel. You know what our weakness is."

"Don't be a smartass, Wilcox. Just spit it out."

Wilcox put his hands to his chest like he'd been shot.

"You wound me, milord. How could little old me be a smartass? And when did you learn such language? The French got their claws into you, didn't they? Filthy frogs."

"You're still a smartass."

Wilcox staggered and put a hand on the hood of a car that was stopped to let them pass. The driver honked and Wilcox actually laid his head on the hood. Another honk and Daniel grabbed him by the back of the jacket and pulled him along.

"My hero," Wilcox said, brushing snow from his forehead. "These New Yorkers are so rude."

"You've got exactly ten seconds to tell me what you want," Daniel said. He stepped onto the sidewalk and merged into the pedestrian stream.

"We can't just hang out? Be pals?"

"Every time we hang out, trouble makes a beeline straight for us."

"Oh, Daniel. You don't need me to find trouble. You're a trouble magnet all by your lonesome."

Again, Wilcox was right on the nose. But that was something Daniel wished to change. He wanted to spend more time with Anna, and that meant not rushing off to save the world every time the world needed saving.

"I'm late."

"For?"

"A very important date," Daniel said.

"Well, look at you. You're trying to be funny. Very good, Daniel. Very good. But may I offer a bit of advice?"

"Not like I could stop you."

Wilcox stopped in the middle of the moving throng.

"Call me when you need me," Wilcox said. His smile went from ear to ear.

"I won't. But thanks."

Wilcox shook his head. "You don't get it, do you? You, me, Cal... we're all the same. We don't have to ask for it. Trouble just finds us. We're bound."

Wilcox disappeared into the crowd. Daniel shook his head. The assassin wasn't wrong. But Daniel was going to do everything in his power to change his fate. He was willing to do the hard work. But it was time to do something for himself. For Anna.

Wilcox could take his trouble and keep it. Daniel wanted none of it.

CHAPTER 5

LOGAN WHITAKER

Logan stared at the computer screen long after his eyes glazed over. He was chasing a story that wasn't there. He'd been mistaken. He must've hit his head. Maybe it was early onset dementia. He thought about calling his mother to ask if he was the only one. Had she ever mentioned a grand-parent who died young and insane?

Logan shook his head and stretched his arms out to the sides. He needed sleep. He'd worked all night and well into the next day.

The most pressing work on his desk was done. It was only two in the afternoon. He should check in with the Mr. Hotshot Reporter. That's what a good low-level peon would do.

"Screw it," he said, closing the laptop and grabbing his coat. If anyone asked, he was going to get lunch.

He made it as far as the elevators. The paper's managing editor, Fiona Graves, appeared with a coffee mug in her hands.

"Logan," she said. Then she gave him an up and down inspection. "When was the last time you slept?"

To tell the truth or not?

"Yesterday, Ms. Graves."

"Here," she said, handing him the coffee. "I haven't had a sip yet. Let's have a word in my office."

Logan wanted to groan and slink away, but he followed his boss to the largest office in the building. Fiona Graves sat on the uncomfortable square couch, and Logan understood he was supposed to sit across from her.

"I only put a little honey in it," she said.

He took a sip. He hated coffee, but nodded anyway. "It's good."

"You're a better liar than you were when we first met, Logan. That means you're learning. You better learn to like coffee if you want to survive in this business. The news cycle's bloodstream runneth brown with coffee. Didn't I tell you that?"

She was trying to be funny, but Logan, despite his desire to stay in her good graces, only nodded.

"Fine. If I can't get a laugh, let's get right to it," she said, folding her hands in her lap. Fiona Graves was an icon in the news business. Her time as a behind-the-lines reporter began during the First Gulf War and ended only recently. She told Logan that she'd only come into a real office kicking and screaming. She was born to wear no makeup and crawl under barbed wire. He believed her. "How are you, Logan? How's your mother?"

Logan took a sip of coffee, trying not to wince. "She's good."

"She still calling you every day?"

"Yes, ma'am."

"That's only natural. I remember when I lost my father. My mother wanted me to move home. I think your mother is much stronger than mine was."

"Yes, ma'am. Thank you."

"I can see that you don't want to talk about personal things, so let's talk about work. How do you think you're faring?"

He'd had occasional check-ins with Graves since beginning at *The Continental Tribune,* but this was her first time asking him how *he* thought he was doing.

"I think I'm doing well, Ms. Graves. The work is hard, but I enjoy it. Never a dull moment."

"Vernon seems to like you."

Vernon Haskins was the Pulitzer Prize Winning Prick.

"He does?"

"You don't think so?" Graves was smiling.

"I guess… well, I…"

"I didn't tell you this when you started. I didn't want to scare you. But Vernon burned through three interns and four budding journalists in the eighteen months before you arrived. The longest lasted a month. Therefore, since you've been here for six months, you win the prize for best pupil."

Logan sighed. "It's a lot harder than I thought. I know I shouldn't say that, but…"

"But you're tired, and some days you wonder why you have to do what you're told to do. Am I close?"

"Yes, ma'am."

"Look, Logan. I know you're not a complainer. I talked to your advisor at Stanford and a couple of your professors. They all gave you high praise for your work ethic and perseverance. But they mentioned one thing that I'd like for you to monitor."

This was news to Logan. He sipped more coffee instead of gulping down his nerves.

"One professor put it succinctly. He said you were stoic to a fault, that you had a hard time asking for help. Do you think that's accurate?"

"You said it yourself, Ms. Graves. I don't like to complain. It's not how my… dad raised me."

"I admire the fact that you want to do right by your parents and your own code. But if you want to last more than a few months in this big, bad city, you're going to have to figure out when it's appropriate to ask for help. Do you understand?"

"Yes, ma'am. I…" He hesitated. He wanted to tell her everything. About Niles Petersen. About Jimmy Mason. About the fact that he thought he was going crazy. He almost told her.

But he didn't.

"I guess it's just gonna take practice," he said instead.

"Good. As long as you hear me. He'd kill me if he knew I was telling you this, but did you know Vernon bounced around to four different newspapers before he finally found his groove? So if he can do it, you can do it. I believe in you, Logan."

"Thank you, ma'am. That means a lot coming from you."

Fiona Graves looked at her watch.

"My time is up. Unless there's anything I can do for you?"

There was.

"Ms. Graves, I think I know the answer, but I'm still trying to figure it all out. The sources we use to confirm stories—"

"You mean the actual people, not the databases?"

"Yes, ma'am. I know each reporter builds their own network of contacts, but is there a service or way to fast track the process?"

Graves nodded and put up a finger. "I see what you're doing."

"You do?"

"Yes. You're getting smart." How does she know what I'm thinking? "You're wondering about how you'll build your own network. Correct?"

Phew!

"Yes, ma'am. I thought I'd get a head start in case there's a chance for me to do my own writing soon."

Graves reached over and pulled a pen and pad from her desk. She scribbled something on the paper, tore it from the pad, and handed it to Logan. He grabbed it, but she held on. "Your first duty is to Vernon."

"Of course."

"If you find time to pursue your own story and your own sources, this firm can help. They're on retainer and supply us with most anything we need."

"Thank you, Ms. Graves. I promise this won't get in the way of my assigned work."

"I know it won't, Logan. Now, unless I am mistaken, I believe you were on your way home to shower and change. Tip from a former all-nighter: keep an extra set of clothes here along with toiletries."

Logan blushed. "Yes, ma'am. Thank you."

The phone on the desk rang and Graves picked it up, waving goodbye.

Logan dumped the quarter-drank coffee in the lounge sink, then put the mug in the dishwasher. He did the same for the discarded mugs in the sink. Logan then hurried to the elevators, and it wasn't until the doors closed that he remembered the piece of paper from Fiona Graves. He read the next clue that he hoped might unravel the Petersen mystery: *Fitzgerald & Muse.*

Knowing Vernon the prick the way he did, Logan guessed the reporter spent little time finding and cultivating his own sources. Maybe this Fitzgerald & Muse was his go-to. At least it was something. Something he would tackle *after* going home to shower.

CHAPTER 6

DANIEL BRIGGS

"How are you?" Cal Stokes asked.

"I'm good. And you? Just run a marathon?"

Daniel watched Cal wipe his face with a white gym towel.

"Trying to keep the edge. Next time we run, I'm beating you."

"We'll see."

Cal picked up his laptop and, for a few moments, the video bounced as he got readjusted. Cal took a long drink from a water bottle. "So what's the plan? You coming home?"

Home, Daniel thought. Did he really have a home?

"I thought I'd hang out in New York for a couple of days. I've never been here for Christmas. It's beautiful."

"No thank you," Cal said. "I'm happy right here. You can keep your big city."

"You could join me. Maybe bring the guys. I'm staying at Jonas's place."

Jonas Layton was officially the CEO of The Jefferson Group. They rarely saw him. Layton was a regular on the speaking circuit because of his status as one of the world's most sought after billionaires, and because he had an uncanny ability to predict world events. Not just because he had more money than he could ever spend in one lifetime, but because he cared about his men, everyone at The Jefferson Group knew that each of Jonas's real estate holdings were at their disposal.

Normally, Daniel would not have availed himself of a luxury like a penthouse with a perfect view of Central Park. But the place was as close to a fortress as he'd find in the city.

"I'm still hoping that Top will be home in time for Christmas. I'm craving his bread pudding."

Top was former Marine Master Sergeant Willie Trent, a giant of a man who could've held his own in the NFL, but instead chose to help save the day and cook the most delicious meals using his world-class culinary skills.

"I ran into a friend today," Daniel said.

"Good friend or bad?"

"The friend who's a bit of both."

"Wilcox. What did he want?"

"He said he was bored."

"A bored Matthew Wilcox is a dangerous Matthew Wilcox."

"My thoughts exactly," Daniel said.

"And he found you, I assume."

"He did."

"How did you leave it?"

"He's not going away."

Cal exhaled and took another swig of water. "What is he up to?"

"I think he was telling the truth. He's bored, and he thinks that if he hangs around one of us long enough, lightning will strike. I don't plan on giving him that opportunity."

"Even more reason for you to come to Charlottesville. Come on. The students are gone. There's no line at Bodo's. We'd have all the bagels for ourselves."

Daniel shook his head. "I can't. Not yet."

Cal looked into the camera. "You're sure you're okay?"

"I am. I promise. Better than I deserve. But I just have this feeling that I need to be here."

Cal leaned back. "You know what Gaucho always says. If Snake Eyes has a feeling, you better listen to that feeling. Or something like that."

Daniel chuckled. "Have he and Top bought a place in the Caribbean yet?"

"Not yet. After our latest dust-up in Cuba, I'd have thought they might look to the mountains. I was wrong. Sounds like they'll pull the trigger soon. Gaucho keeps talking about the big party he's gonna throw."

"Sounds like fun," Daniel said. "I've missed you all."

"We've missed you, my friend." Cal picked up his phone and waggled it. "I've ignored five calls since we've been on. Let me let you go. But call if you need us. Okay?"

"I will."

Cal nodded, and his face disappeared from Daniel's screen.

Christmas in Charlottesville was tempting. But Daniel knew he had to be right here, right now. Why? He didn't know. Maybe he'd find out soon. The old senses were coming back. The Beast inside him stirred. *Soon,* he thought. *Soon.*

CHAPTER 7

LOGAN WHITAKER - FITZGERALD & MUSE

"Mr. Whitaker?" a scrawny man with a five o'clock shadow said as he stepped into the small waiting room.

Logan stood. "That's me." He was nervous. He'd showered, shaved, tried to take a quick nap and failed. Then he'd forced himself to drink more coffee and come here just before closing. It was a trick he'd learned early on at *The Continental Tribune*: when you wanted something bad enough, get there first or last. He hadn't understood why at the time, probably something to do with psychology, but it worked.

"Technically, we're closing in fifteen minutes, Mr. Whitaker, but considering your employer..."

We must pay you a lot of money, Logan thought. This guy looked like a rule follower.

"I won't take much of your time. I was just hoping to better understand your process, as I build my own list of sources."

The man's eyes went from dull to intrigued. No doubt, he

saw Logan's request as a way for the firm to make more money from their client.

"I'm Marty Muse. Co-Founder of Fitzgerald and Muse."

Logan shook the man's hand.

"Logan Whitaker, Mr. Muse."

"Follow me. I'll give you the dime tour."

There wasn't much to see. Compared to Logan's employer, Fitzgerald & Muse was tiny. He counted two larger offices. Both could fit together in Fiona Graves's office with room to spare. There was a small library with soundproof booths for privacy. When they walked back to the secretary's desk, she was gone for the day.

"What is your background, Mr. Muse?" Logan asked.

"I was once a journalist, like you. I had a knack for cultivating sources. It was my partner, Ian Fitzgerald, the man you saw in one office, who said we should strike out on our own. Now we supply New York, D.C., Los Angeles and various foreign postings with sources to corroborate ongoing news pieces."

"Is there a lot of money in source sourcing?"

"You go straight for the throat, don't you, Logan?"

Logan flushed. "I'm sorry, I didn't mean to—"

Muse laughed. "It's fine. And refreshing. And in case you were wondering, we prefer to call our services *Source Acquisition*. And yes, we make a fair bit of money. Nothing astronomical. As a liaison and introductory agent between vetted sources and media outlets, we see it as our duty to maintain the highest caliber of transparency. I'm sure Vernon's told you all about the duty of journalistic integrity."

"He has. At length."

Muse laughed again. "I could tell you stories about Vernon, but I won't." He made a zipping his lips gesture. "Much like attorney client privilege, we take our role as intermediaries seriously. I'm sure you can understand why."

"Yes, I do. So how does it work? Do you build a portfolio

of sources for a reporter based on personality and need, or is it a story-by-story kind of thing?"

"I'll give you the canned answer: it depends. If a reporter like Vernon Haskins comes to us, and we know the arenas in which he treads, it's fairly easy to cobble together sources he might need. Now, it's up to the sources to provide the information, not us. We in no way guarantee the end result. We merely guarantee the validity and standing of the source."

"Do you ever get rid of a source?"

"Yes. They're only human, after all. My job is to find them, and present them. If a source is no longer presentable, say there's been a history of complaints, or if they've moved on to a role not conducive to our needs, we evaluate whether said source should be removed from our offerings."

Logan nodded. "Why do sources do it? Can they be compensated?"

"I'll repeat what I said before: it depends. Our clients often compensate industry experts, researchers, celebrities. Then we have the whistleblowers, the anonymous sources who wish to remain nameless. That's a stickier situation and one where we advise clients to tread carefully. If compensation compromises the credibility of the reporting, we recommend excluding compensation from the relationship."

Logan glanced at his watch. "Last question, Mr. Muse. How many sources who don't get compensated would you say do it out of the kindness of their heart, some feeling of altruism, versus the possibility of personal gain?"

Muse grinned. "Asked like a true journalist. While I am very good at what I do, I am not a human lie detector. You might say that every source has something to gain. While I am far from a pessimist, I understand human nature. I know people can twist stories. We each have our flaws and leanings. That's why journalistic integrity necessitates the use of multiple sources to corroborate any story that our clients put out into the world. The manner in which they do is up to them."

Logan took a chance. He pulled out the crumpled paper with Vernon's sources listed.

"Do you recognize the people on this list?" he asked.

Marty Muse looked at the paper.

"This is Vernon's."

"It is."

"He gave it to you?"

"I had to confirm the details of the recent incident at the border."

"Nasty business. I hope they get it sorted out. And yes, I recognize those names. All but one are ours."

"Can you tell me which one?"

Muse shook his head. "Why don't you ask Vernon. Now, it's well past closing, and my wife is expecting me. If you have more questions, why don't you come by during working hours? If you couldn't tell, I can talk about our services for hours."

Muse escorted Logan to the stairs and said a quick goodbye. As he made his way down the four flights, Logan replayed the conversation in his head, every gesture. Marty Muse seemed to tell the truth. But was that just because he was very good at lying, or because Logan had come to the wrong place looking for answers?

IAN FITZGERALD

"Headed home, Marty?" Ian Fitzgerald asked from his office. Their desks faced one another from across the hall. It was a habit from the old days in the newsroom.

"That's right. Mary has a pot roast in the slow cooker. She'll kill me if I'm late."

"Who was the kid?"

"Works for Vernon over at *The Continental,*" Muse said, gathering his laptop and keys.

"Poor kid. What did he want?"

"He's new. Wanted to better understand what we do, how we service his paper."

"I wish more of the newbies would do that."

"Me, too." Muse walked across the hall and stuck his head into Fitzgerald's office. "Vernon has him running around confirming with sources."

"Sounds like Vernon. If he can pawn off the work, he will. Did he say what the story was?"

"Once a reporter, always a reporter," Muse said.

"Guilty."

"It was about that thing at the border. You know, the cartel tunnels and dead immigrants."

Ian Fitzgerald clenched his fists in his lap. "Nasty business."

"That's what I said. I've gotta run. Have a good night, Ian."

"You too, Marty. Tell Mary I said hello."

Muse left and Ian Fitzgerald swiveled around in his chair. He knew all about the aforementioned story. He also knew about Niles Petersen and that there'd been some young guy at the scene. Ian Fitzgerald also knew about the stabbing and the replacement Niles Petersen. He knew because he was the one who'd set it all up.

Now, he had to figure out what this kid from *The Continental Ledger* was really doing here, and if he was the same kid from the night before.

CHAPTER 8

DANIEL BRIGGS

One thing he and Anna had done on his recuperative leave was watch movies. When Anna first suggested they snuggle up on the couch and "veg out," Daniel prepared himself for Hollywood Classics. Or maybe foreign films considering her lifestyle.

He was wrong.

It turned out that Anna loved eighties and nineties movies. They watched a slew of Arnold Schwarzenegger flicks. She especially liked *Kindergarten Cop* and *Twins*. They even went back and watched all the Conan movies. For a day, Anna recited the same line over and over in Conan's voice: "To see my enemies driven before me, and hear the lamentation of their women." She did a fair Austrian accent.

He missed Anna, and when he saw the advertisement for a late night marathon of eighties movies at an independent movie theater, he took the chance.

The theater was a block away when he looked across the street and saw a young man coming out of an office building. It was the same guy from the train station, the one with his head in his hands. Daniel noticed the bags under the young man's eyes, but there was a determination in his step that made the former sniper cross the street and follow a safe distance behind.

They passed the theater and the line of moviegoers that ran down the block. The wind howled and snow did its best to add to the accumulation of slush on the road.

Why are you following this kid? Daniel asked himself.

He knew why. He was having one of 'those' feelings again, the old instincts kicking in. Daniel didn't think the young man was the cause of trouble, but he could be in trouble. Might as well follow for a bit. It couldn't hurt. Could it?

If the guy was in trouble, it must not be bad, because he never looked back. That gave Daniel a chance to get as close as he dared, always ready to duck into a doorway or turn to avoid detection.

Two blocks turned to five, and still the young man hurried. A crowd of partygoers with baby blue pinwheel hats got between them, and for a second Daniel thought he'd lost his mark. Then he saw the young man turn left and go into the tallest building on the block. Daniel read the sign: *The Continental Ledger*.

He passed by the building and saw the guy wave a pass at the aging security guard. Daniel kept walking, then turned around. There was still time to catch the first movie. But the pull was too strong. He was supposed to be here, now.

Daniel leaned against a brick wall and pretended to scroll through his phone, all the while monitoring the streets for anything out of the ordinary. Nothing. Just New Yorkers going about their night. Fifteen minutes turned to thirty, then sixty. Still nothing.

It was cold and getting colder.

He was just looking up at the lull in the weather when a car pulled to the curb across the street from the newspaper building and a man stepped out, saying something to the driver. The car sped off, and the man cut his way across traffic.

He felt the man's gaze pass over him, and for a split second thought the man was here for him. The Beast in Daniel coiled, ready. But the man's gaze, though wary, slipped past and settled on *The Continental Ledger*. He walked inside and Daniel moved closer so he could see what the man was doing. Daniel saw the reflection of the cop's badge flashed at the security guard. When the guard went to pick up the phone, the cop shook his head and said something. The phone went back on the desk and the two men had words. Daniel watched and wished he could hear.

Finally, the security guard said something, and the cop walked to the elevators and disappeared.

You're imagining things, Daniel told himself. *Don't get involved.*

Too late. He couldn't help it. He was walking through the front doors before he had a chance to turn back.

"May I help you, sir?" the security guard asked. Daniel didn't think the old timer could catch a thief if his life depended on it.

"The cop that just came in here…"

"Officer Francisco," the security guard offered.

"I think so," Daniel said. "I just gave him a lift over and he left his phone in my car." He held his own phone up in the air.

He could see the security guard trying to figure out what to do. Daniel prodded. "Look, my grandmother is expecting me for a late dinner. I don't want to disappoint her. I just need to give the phone back."

"Why don't you leave it with me?" the security guard offered, wincing when he shifted off his left leg.

"The phone's been ringing since he left my car. What if it's an emergency, like a murder or something?" Daniel said, playing up the act.

The security guard's thoughts were all over his face.

"I could get in a lot of trouble—"

"Sir, I'm just trying to do the right thing. Tell me where the officer went and I'll run up there, give him the phone, and be out of here before you can say Captain Kangaroo."

"Ha. Captain Kangaroo. Loved that guy." More thinking. "Fine. But if you don't come right back down—"

"I promise," Daniel said, holding up the phone, which was ringing again.

The security guard waved him in. "Sixth floor. The cop was looking for Logan Whitaker. Cubicles are on the left as you step out, then right a ways."

"Thanks!"

Daniels hustled to the elevator. This could all be a mistake. If it was, he'd find another way out. If it wasn't a mistake, Daniel would handle that, too.

CHAPTER 9

LOGAN WHITAKER

Logan logged into his computer and started doing what he should've done first; look up the names of Vernon's sources. Niles Petersen came first. The database the newspaper employed said that Niles Petersen was currently a mid-level manager with a government entity tied to the Department of Immigration. He did not recognize the organization. There were no pictures, which seemed strange - but maybe not as rare as Logan assumed.

He'd come back to Petersen.

He typed in Jimmy Mason. The database came up with forty-three hits. When he narrowed the search to the city, there were three hits. Logan scanned each file quickly.

The first Jimmy Mason was actually a mason. He specialized in stone work and his Yelp reviews said he was usually on time, but sometimes took long lunches.

The second Jimmy Mason was deceased and had been unemployed for nine years before his passing. There was even a picture of the program from this Mason's funeral.

The third Jimmy Mason was loading when a voice startled Logan.

"Mr. Whitaker?"

Logan turned and saw a man holding up a badge. It only took him a second to recognize the man.

"You're the cop from the stabbing," Logan said, the words blurting out before he could stop them.

"Officer Francisco," the cop said.

"I waited like you told me."

The cop cocked his head to one side. "They never showed?"

"No, officer."

"Huh. That's weird."

"And when I called, they said they didn't have a record of Niles Petersen at all."

"Now that I can explain. We were swamped. Hospitals were filled to the gills. Had to take the poor guy across town. By the time we filed the report, it was this afternoon. And I think you got the name wrong."

"I'm sorry?" Logan said.

"You said Petersen. The guy's name was Hanson, like the band." The cop chuckled good-naturedly.

"No, I'm sure his name was Niles Petersen. I talked to him."

The cop stepped closer. "Trust me, kid, I filed the report. The guy's name was Hanson. Kevin Hanson. Look it up."

"I will. Wait, so why are you here?"

"I'm cleaning up my mess. I should've taken you with us, but they told me they were sending another car. So now I've gotta take you down to the station and get your statement."

"How did you find me? I never gave you my name."

The cop stepped closer. He put his hand on Logan's desk. His breath smelled of stale coffee masked with peppermint.

"Yes, you did. You don't remember. It happens. You were scared. But it's okay, kid. I promise you're not in trouble."

Logan was feeling like he was very much in trouble.

"I've got a lot of work to do. Can you take my statement here?"

The cop shook his head. "Part of the mess. My lieutenant says I have to bring you in. His rules, not mine."

If only Vernon the prick had walked by at just that moment. But almost everybody was gone because of Christmas. The news never stopped, but Christmas still slowed late night work at *The Continental*.

"Officer, how about I promise to come down to the station tomorrow?" He pointed to the pile of papers. "I'm the low man on the totem pole. If I don't get a jump on this, there's no way my boss is gonna let me go home for Christmas."

Logan watched the cop's face change, fully expecting the soft game to go hard. The cop didn't get the chance. Someone said, "Officer Francisco?"

At first the cop didn't turn. Then a warning light went off in the cop's eyes and his head shifted.

"Yes?"

All Logan could see of the newcomer was a blonde ponytail. "Officer, the guard downstairs said your driver called."

"He did?"

"Yes, sir. Says something about an emergency."

"You sure?"

Logan saw hands go up in an exasperated gesture. "I'm just here, like Logan, to get my work done before Christmas. My stack is twice as high as his. You think I wanna be passing on messages right now?"

"Okay. Thanks," the cop said. He turned back to Logan. "I'll be back to get you in the morning. Eight o'clock sharp, got it?"

"Yes, sir."

Logan watched the cop go, then stood to thank the stranger. When he opened his mouth, his eyes went wide.

"You."

It was the guy from the train station.

The man put a finger to his lips and motioned back to the elevators where Officer Francisco was pulling out his phone. The blonde man snagged the chair from the next cubicle and sat down. "I think we've got two minutes tops before he figures out that his driver didn't call and that he really wants to talk to you now."

"Who the hell are you?"

The man put up his hands in a 'I mean no harm' gesture.

"My name is Daniel. And I've got a feeling you have a story to tell."

"How do you know that?" Logan moved to leave, and the stranger grabbed his forearm.

"I don't know much, Logan. But I do know the look of a man who's in trouble."

"How?"

"Because I was that man for a long time."

Logan sat down to face Daniel. It almost all came out right then and there.

"I don't know what to do," he whispered.

"Then let me help you."

For some reason, Logan felt he could trust this man. Maybe it was desperation. Or maybe it was the look in the man's eyes. He couldn't be certain. But when Daniel asked him where the back stairs were, Logan led the way, having the distinct feeling that his life would never be the same.

CHAPTER 10

LOGAN WHITAKER

"Where are we going?" Logan asked as they stepped out of the back exit of the building.

"To watch," Daniel replied, looking left and right casually.

"You've done this before."

"A few times."

Logan couldn't help but say, "How do I know you're not kidnapping me?"

Daniel stopped and looked at him. "You can leave any time you'd like."

"You're serious."

"Of course."

"If it matters, I didn't think you were going to kidnap me."

"How?"

"You don't have the look."

That elicited a chuckle from the pony-tailed man.

"What's funny?" Logan asked.

"You should've seen me a few months ago. I'm not sure you would've said the same thing."

Instead of explaining, Daniel motioned down the alley and led the way around the building. When they'd gotten to the corner, Daniel pointed.

"See them?"

Logan had to squint through the swirling snow, but he saw them.

"Officer Francisco," he said.

"If that's his real name."

"Who's the other guy?"

"I was hoping you'd know."

"I can't be for sure. It's too far, but I don't think I know that person either."

They watched as the two men had words. Officer Francisco spoke into his phone, and then they loaded into the sedan and zoomed down the street, the back end fishtailing in the slush.

"You hungry?" Daniel asked.

"Not really. Why?"

"We need to go somewhere to talk."

"How about my place?" Logan said.

"I appreciate your trust, Logan, but until you know me and I know what's coming after you, I think it's best that we stick to public places. Agreed?"

"Sure. Good idea."

What is it about this man? Logan thought. He'd just met Daniel, but Logan could already tell that he would follow the man's calm determination almost anywhere.

"Eggs, over easy. Bacon. And coffee. Black, please," Daniel said to the waitress.

"I'll have the same." Logan still wasn't hungry, but he thought he should make an effort.

When the waitress left, Logan tried to find the next right question to ask. He had so many.

"Aren't you going to ask me what all this is about?" Logan asked.

"I figured you'd tell me when you were ready."

"I'm ready."

Daniel nodded. "Let's wait for the coffee. You look like you need it. When was the last time you slept?"

"I don't know. Forty-eight hours?"

"How much steam do you have left?"

"I'm running on adrenaline right now. I can't get Officer Francisco out of my head."

"Okay. Let's start there. How did you meet him?"

The waitress appeared with two coffee mugs and a carafe. She set them on the table and went back to the kitchen.

Daniel poured the coffee and slid a mug to Logan. "It's hot."

Logan nodded, gathering his thoughts. He needed to tell someone.

"The reporter I work for, Vernon Haskins, sent me to confirm details with his sources. The first source on the list was a man named Niles Petersen. I met him outside his home. That's when things got interesting…"

They'd polished their first coffee and were starting in on food when Logan finished the story. Daniel hadn't said a word, but Logan could see the older man processing the information.

"What do you think?" Logan asked, very much wanting to know what the man sitting across from him thought of the last two days of Logan's life.

"I think you stepped in something you weren't supposed to step in."

"You think I'm in danger?"

"I think you know the answer to that question."

Logan looked down at his food.

"Eat," Daniel said.

Logan ate, slowly at first. With each bite, his body turned

more ravenous. The next time he looked up, Daniel was still eating and Logan's plate was empty.

"Feel better?" Daniel asked.

"A little."

"Want more?"

"Not yet." Logan pushed the plate to the edge of the table, and the ever efficient waitress quickly scooped it up and out of the way before anyone could ask. "I'm scared."

"You should be," Daniel said.

"You think I'm a coward?"

"You're a smart guy. I think you know the difference between being scared and being a coward. A coward would've caved in to Officer Francisco. A coward wouldn't chalk up everything that's happened to being crazy. You didn't give in. You kept pulling the string to unravel the mystery."

"So maybe I'm just stupid."

Daniel grinned. "If I called myself stupid for every time I pulled the string... Logan, there are some things to consider. First, your safety. It might be better to just let these guys have what they want and live to fight another day."

"You're saying we should let them get away with this, whatever *this* is?"

"I didn't say that. I said we need to consider your safety."

"You don't strike me as a safety guy, Daniel."

Another grin. "I'd like to know what's going on. You don't make a body disappear unless there's something to hide; maybe something big. I have the experience to tackle this, and have a place you can stay until—"

"No way. I'm coming with you."

"Even if it means getting chased, shot at, and maybe killed?"

"You're trying to scare me," Logan said.

"Is it working?"

"A little."

Daniel forked his last piece of egg. "Good. A healthy sense of fear will keep you alive. Now, let's talk about Fitzgerald & Muse. How can we get—"

The shrill ring of Logan's phone cut in and Logan said, "Sorry. It's my roommate. Maybe I should get it."

"Go ahead. You want anything else?"

"Pancakes?"

Daniel motioned for the waitress while Logan answered the call.

"Hey, Sam. What's up?"

"Logan, there's a couple of cops here that want to talk to you."

Daniel had obviously heard, because he was staring at Logan. He held the phone off his ear so Daniel could listen.

"What do they want?"

"Something about an attack. It sounds serious, man."

Sam was a mild-mannered kid from Oklahoma City. He was neat, quiet and worked four out of five days from home. He was the exact opposite of confrontational.

"Can you tell them I'm out on a story?"

Logan listened to Sam tell them. He could not hear their response.

"They say they need to talk to you."

"No problem," Logan said. "Tell them I'll be in touch when I'm done. I was supposed to meet Officer Francisco at eight tomorrow morning."

More murmuring in the background, and Sam said.

"Officer Francisco says it can't wait. He needs you to come home now."

Logan looked at Daniel, who, after a moment, nodded.

Logan tried to keep his voice calm and reassuring when he answered. "Okay, Sam. I'll be home soon."

The call ended, and Logan stared at the phone.

"Shit."

"It's okay, Logan."

Logan was going to ask Daniel about Sam, about what the hell they were going to do. But when he looked up into Daniel's eyes, he almost jumped up in shock. The man's eyes had gone from calm to dancing with fire.

"I don't understand," Logan stuttered.

"They ramped up the pressure, Logan. And pressure is where I work best."

Logan didn't doubt him. Not with the way he'd suddenly transformed into something new, something almost sinister to Logan's eyes. But when Daniel put a hundred-dollar bill on the table and walked to the door, Logan followed him.

CHAPTER 11

LOGAN WHITAKER

"You're sure we should do this?" Logan asked, punching in the code to his building.

"Like we discussed. I'm a colleague. We're working on a story together. You didn't want to talk to them alone."

"And you're sure you want to risk coming with me?"

Daniel smiled. "I'm fine."

He looked fine, like he was heading to the mall, not walking into an ambush against a couple of crooked cops.

"Okay." Logan pushed the door open, and they headed for the stairs like Daniel had instructed.

"When we get to your apartment, let me go in first," Daniel said.

Logan swallowed down his nerves and led the way up to the fifth floor. He felt winded and hadn't realized he had been holding his breath. "It's that one. Five oh nine."

Daniel pushed past him and tried the door. It opened without a key. The man with the blonde ponytail and fiery eyes walked in, Logan a few steps behind.

"Officer Francisco. Nice to see you again," Daniel said. "And you must be Sam."

Sam was sitting on a kitchen stool against the island. Sam didn't reply, just looked at Logan like this was all his fault and all Sam wanted to do was run.

"Mr. Whitaker, we need to speak to you alone," Officer Francisco said. His partner, a sneering guy with a lazy eye, stood off to the side, a badge clipped to his belt.

"Sam, why don't you take a walk?" Daniel said.

Sam sprang to his feet.

"Hold on, pal. You're not the one giving orders around here," Officer Francisco said.

Daniel didn't back down. "And I didn't know this was an inquisition. Sam, you can go."

Whether Daniel's bravado surprised the cops, or it was an easy way for another witness to be gone, Logan couldn't know. He had yet to say a word, and that was just fine with him.

Sam gave Logan a quick look, grabbed his coat and keys, and rushed out the door.

"Besides being Logan's colleague, I am also a practicing attorney. So why don't you tell me what all this is about, gentlemen?"

The two cops exchanged a look. The second man nodded, as if to say, "Tell them."

Officer Fransisco said, "We'd like to talk to Mr. Whitaker about his connection to a murder."

"You mean Niles Petersen," Daniel said.

"No. The man's name was Kevin Hanson."

"You sure it wasn't Devin? Or maybe Galvin?"

"No. His name was Kevin Hanson."

Daniel nodded earnestly. "Here's the problem, gentlemen. There's no record of a Kevin Hanson being murdered last night."

Logan tensed. This wasn't something they'd discussed. What was Daniel doing?

"That's probably because we haven't released that information to the public yet," Officer Francisco replied cooly.

"It wasn't public records that we checked, officer. It was the official police record. Still no mention of Kevin Hanson. No mention of Logan Whitaker either."

"You're impeding an active investigation. And I didn't catch your name Mr.—"

"That's because I didn't give it," Daniel said. His tone had never once wavered from polite.

"Why don't you let me crack this hippy over the head with my pistol," the second cop said, adjusting his coat so Logan could see the weapon in its holster.

"I'd like to see you try," Daniel replied. This time, his tone was cool and hard as steel. Logan couldn't see his face, but something in the cops' body language changed. Then they both went for their weapons.

"Hands up! Both of you!" Officer Francisco yelled.

Logan's hands shot up in the air. Daniel's did not.

"I said, hands in the air!"

"No problem," Daniel said. "But first, tell me why you killed Niles Petersen."

The second cop actually laughed. "Can you believe this son of a bitch? He's ballsy alright."

"Answer the question," Daniel said. He hadn't moved.

Officer Francisco stepped close enough to put his pistol in Daniel's face.

"You reporters don't know when to quit, do you? Well, you're about to find out what happened to Niles Petersen. So help me I—"

It happened quickly. Daniel's hand snapped up, snatched the gun from the Officer Francisco's hand, and whipped him across the head, knocking him to the ground. Daniel stepped forward, pistol extended, pointed straight at the second cop.

"You're messing with the wrong guys," the man said.

"I could say the same about you," Daniel replied. "Put the gun down. Now."

The cop's hand was shaking. "You're crazy."

Logan couldn't be sure, but he thought he saw Daniel's eyes flick to the window. There was a shattering of glass, and when Logan's eyes went back to Daniel and the still-standing officer, the cop had a neat hole in the side of his head and his brains had splattered against the apartment wall. Logan watched in slow motion as the man crumpled to the floor.

CHAPTER 12

LOGAN WHITAKER

Time sped up. Logan was staring at the body on the ground when more glass shattered and he saw the body of Officer Francisco convulse three times. Red spots. Each on the torso. Then he felt someone pulling him out the door.

"Logan. We have to run."

Whose voice was it?

Oh, yeah. Daniel.

Reluctantly, his legs started moving, though his feet felt like lead weights.

Daniel dragged him away from the bloodbath. His mind tried to put together what he'd seen. There were shots. Four in total. Glass breaking. The sound was faint, like a tinkling of bells in the distance. No loud booms like you hear in the movies.

They went the back fire escape. Logan vaguely understood that Daniel was looking all around. Should he be frightened?

I'm in shock, Logan thought. He'd never been in shock,

except for when his father died. An image of his father came to him. A memory from years before. On a farm. Learning how to shoot. He said Logan was a natural. Logan felt pride.

"Just remember," his father had said. "Never point your weapon at anything you don't intend to shoot."

His mind snapped back to the present. Without remembering how, they were walking arm in arm down a side street, their feet kicking through almost six inches of snow.

"You with me?" Daniel asked. He kept his eyes downcast, shielded from the cascading snow.

"Yeah. I'm okay."

They didn't speak again for two blocks. When they did, Daniel pulled him behind a burned-out hulk of a building that might've been a restaurant once.

"What happened?" Logan asked. "Who... I mean, how..."

"I don't know," Daniel said. "How do you feel about coming to my place?"

"Is it safe?"

"It is."

"I just remembered. Sam. What are we going to do about Sam?"

"Pull up his number."

Logan scrolled through his contacts and clicked on Sam's profile. "You want me to call him?"

"Let me do it," Daniel said, grabbing the phone and placing the call.

"Hello? Logan?"

"I'm here with Logan, Sam. My name is Daniel. We met briefly at your apartment."

"Are the cops gone? Is it safe to go back?"

"Do you have another place you can stay?"

There was a pause and then Sam said, "Uh, sure. I was planning on asking a co-worker if I could crash on his couch."

"Good. You do that. Once you're there, don't leave."

"Is Logan okay?"

"Logan's fine. Tell him, Logan."

Logan leaned closer and said, "I'm good, Sam. Do what Daniel tells you."

"Okay," Sam said. Logan could imagine him whispering into his phone in a nook of an all-night bodega.

"Text us the address where you'll be staying. After I text back, power down your phone. Don't make any calls. Stay offline. Understand?" Daniel said.

"I think so. How long do you think—"

"I don't know. We'll be in touch as soon as we can."

Daniel ended the call, waited for Sam's text, then powered down Logan's phone.

"Come on," Daniel said. "While you get some sleep, I'm going to find out who did this."

CHAPTER 13

IAN FITZGERALD

"You really should talk to my wine man, Fitzy. He can get you the best in the world."

Gregory Worthington, in his slick and tailored London suit, swirled the red wine in his glass and watched it stick, then cascade down the inside of the expensive vessel.

Ian Fitzgerald did what he always did when his old friend talked down to him. He ignored the jab and played along.

"Send me his information. I can't seem to find anything worth drinking in the city."

"The city. I don't know how you stand it. New York is so 1995. Why don't you go somewhere fun, like Los Angeles or Copenhagen?"

Gregory Worthington and Ian had gone to prep school together. Gregory was the fourth generation in his family to attend Hawthorne Crest Preparatory. The Worthingtons had somehow kept and grown their wealth over the preceding one hundred years. The curse of the second and third generations was not part of the Worthington DNA.

Ian's last name at the time was Fitzgibbons, from his father's family. His father taught English Literature at Hawthorne Crest Academy. His position afforded his only son discounted tuition, and father and son stayed in quarters furnished by the school. Young Gregory and Ian had met their first day of school, when they'd become roommates. It wasn't until after graduation from college that Gregory pressured his friend to change his last name to Fitzgerald.

"It sounds so much more distinguished," Worthington had said.

Ian Fitzgerald rose from the leather chair and walked to the bar. He selected his favorite scotch and poured them each a glass. When he handed one to Gregory, the now head of the Worthington fortune said, "Who do you have to talk to about upping the decor in this place? Just say the word and I'll get you an invitation to my club."

Ian knew that Gregory's club came with a seven-figure initiation fee, dues that cost more than most CEOs made, and a list of standards that royalty might struggle to achieve.

"I like my club," Ian said. "It's cozy, and close to home."

Gregory looked around the private room. "If you say so." His gaze went back to Ian. "Fitzy, how's business? Is my investment growing or do I need to tell my accounting team that it's going to be another wash?"

There were days that Ian regretted ever taking a penny from his rich friend. He'd taken the investment because the only real strings attached were Gregory's occasional interrogation and condescension.

"I'm glad you asked."

Gregory sat up straighter. "Do tell."

Ian gave him a brief rundown of what he expected Fitzgerald & Muse to net by the end of the year. It was officially their first year in the black. That meant he didn't have to go to Gregory and ask for more money. He hated that part of the arrangement.

Gregory nodded. "And do you expect this growth to continue?"

"Actually, I have something better. Call it a bonus return on your investment."

"An early Christmas present?"

"If you'd like."

Gregory actually looked intrigued. That made Ian feel more pleased than he cared to admit. Their relationship had always been one-sided. Billions in the bank had the right to tip the scales.

"Nicholas La Roche," Ian said.

Gregory's face turned sour.

"I told you never to mention that bastard's name in my presence."

"How would you like to know what the La Roche family is up to?"

"I don't think I care."

The La Roche clan and the Worthingtons had been rivals since the Great Depression. In the early 1900s, Julian La Roche transformed his family's fortune, turning their canned food import business into a food manufacturing empire. Meanwhile, the Worthingtons struggled to keep their agriculture concerns from crumbling. There'd been some long-forgotten spat that seemed to grow in importance over the years. There wasn't a newspaper article or news report that didn't mention one family without mentioning the other. The competitors appeared locked in a never-ending feud that shifted with changing tides and evolving economies.

"You don't care that the La Roches are about to consolidate all their North American operations under one brand as soon as they buy controlling interest of Gamber Pharmaceuticals?"

"What?! How do you know that?"

"It's my business to know. *Our* business to know, Gregory."

Ian sipped his favorite scotch and watched as his friend's mind spun off on the possibility. When he finally came to, he said exactly what Ian knew he would say. "We can easily increase our holdings in Gamber and force them to sell to us. That would send La Roche through the roof! How long have you been holding this, Fitzy?"

"We got final confirmation yesterday."

Gregory swirled his drink absentmindedly. "We knew they were consolidating, but not like this. Buying Gamber would put them ahead. Even if we can't buy Gamber outright, we'll use our people at the DOJ to sue them until they say uncle."

"I'm glad the information will prove helpful," Ian said, smiling.

"Helpful? This is monumental. This is…" Gregory's eyes locked on Ian's. "What do you want, Fitzy?"

"Isn't it enough to see my friend happy?"

"Don't give me that, Fitzy. I've known you since before you tasted beer. You're planning something, aren't you?"

Ian Fitzgerald had thought hard about how much to tell his friend. He'd realized long ago that it was impossible to amass a fortune like the Worthingtons. It was only when he'd befriended his partner, Marty Muse, that he understood that there was a unique power in the world that even the Worthingtons and the La Roches didn't fully control: information. It was through brokering information that Ian Fitzgerald would build his legacy.

"I hoped you might introduce me to some of your friends."

"Which friends?" Gregory asked.

"The ones who have enemies."

Ian saw the lightbulb go off.

"Ah. Now I see. How long have you been planning this, Fitzy? A long time?"

"Longer than you could ever imagine," Ian said, lifting his glass to his friend.

What Ian didn't say was that his real vision had always been to step on, then over, his good friend, Gregory. That was how the world worked. And that was exactly what Ian Fitzgerald planned to do.

CHAPTER 14

LOGAN WHITAKER

They skirted Central Park. The snow was finally making New Yorkers hunker down. The streets were nearly deserted. Daniel led them to a shiny tower that sat with an unobstructed view of the park.

Instead of going through the front door, Daniel swiped a card at the garage entry. They wound their way through a space loaded with every imaginable brand of luxury automobile. Instead of the card, Daniel put his hand on a scanner at the elevator. In a soft female voice, the elevator said, "Welcome. I hope you're having a pleasant night."

Logan laughed.

"If only she knew."

"It's good that you're laughing," Daniel said. "You want to talk about what happened?"

"Not yet. I'm still processing. And by the way you led us here, I'm assuming you have a plan."

"I do."

"Then, if you don't mind, I'd love to take a shower and have a drink."

Logan watched as the elevator rose to the top flour labeled PENTHOUSE.

"How many units are up here?" Logan asked.

"Just one."

"Your place?"

"A friend's," Daniel said.

The elevator opened to a wide hallway. The door up ahead was massive and looked like it belonged at Fort Knox, not next to Central Park. There was no handle. Just a button in the middle of the door. Daniel pressed it.

There was a pause. Then the door spoke in a man's voice. "Welcome, Daniel."

The door opened on its own, and when it did, the thickness of the thing gave the impression of a bank vault.

"What is this place?" Logan asked.

"I told you, my friend's apartment."

"This isn't an apartment, Daniel. This is a mansion at the top of a skyscraper."

Logan looked all around as Daniel led him inside. The door closed behind them without a sound.

This place is soundproof, Logan thought.

"You want a drink or shower first?" Daniel asked.

"Shower, please."

They walked through a modern living area that could've hosted a party of at least a hundred people. They passed floor to ceiling windows and Logan looked down at Central Park.

"Wow," he said.

"Pretty amazing, right?"

"I don't know if amazing is a good enough word."

He tore himself from the view and followed past the massive kitchen and down a hall that was as wide as his own apartment was big. They passed an office and a pair of bedrooms.

Daniel stopped at the last bedroom on the right.

"Shower's in on the left. The closet is right off the bathroom. Throw your clothes in the hamper and pick whatever you want to wear. I'll be in the kitchen."

Logan had so many questions, but the thought of shower was more powerful. He felt like he was covered in blood.

The bedroom was vast, and the bathroom was modern and luxurious. He turned on the shower and walked to the closet. The lights flickered on automatically, and Logan's eyes went wide. There was row upon row of clothing. All new. Someone had tagged each article with a description and size, ranging from medium up to XXL.

He chose TSHIRT-BLACK and JEANS-BLUE-32x32. He snagged some boxer briefs and Smartwool socks, stripped down, and tossed his dirty clothes into the hamper.

The water in the shower was powerful and rejuvenating. He stood in the stream for a time and wished that the last two days would just wash away down the drain. Then he scrubbed himself down with the expensive and gloriously perfumed body soap and shampoo. Clear-headed now, Logan wondered who Daniel's friend was. For that matter, he wondered who Daniel was. There wasn't a moment since they'd met that the man didn't look at ease and completely in control.

He left the shower reluctantly, toweled off with the fluffiest towel he'd ever held, dressed, and went to find Daniel. There was an open beer on the kitchen counter. Logan picked it up and took a sip. He heard talking coming from the living room.

When he found Daniel, he was sitting across from a man wearing a t-shirt that said, "Jersey Is Better Than Manhattan." They both looked up when Logan entered the room.

"Look at you, so fresh and so clean," the man in the t-shirt said. Logan could feel the man appraising him, and he didn't like the way it felt. His look was more accusation than inspection.

"Logan, I'd like for you to meet a—"

"He's going to say friend, I promise. Weren't you, Daniel?"

For the first time, Logan thought he caught annoyance in Daniel's gaze.

"This is Matthew. Matthew, this is Logan Whitaker."

Matthew rose and shook Logan's hand. "So you're the naughty little reporter with two rotting corpses in his apartment." Logan almost dropped his beer. Matthew laughed. "You should see the look on your face, kid. Daniel, are you seeing this?"

"Leave him alone," Daniel said.

Matthew hadn't let go of Logan's hand. "I'm serious, Logan. Two corpses. Both rotting. I wonder if the blood's seeped through your carpet, into the hardwoods, and down into the apartment below yours. What do you think?"

Logan yanked his hand back. "I think I'd better finish this beer before I answer you."

Matthew guffawed. "Maybe you aren't a worm of a reporter. I like you, Logan. I really do." The strange man sat back down on the couch. "So, now that we're all here, should we hand out the power rings and pronounce our unity?"

Logan sat down nearer to Daniel.

"Is he always like this?" Logan asked.

"Always," Daniel replied.

"If you don't like it, you know I can leave," Matthew said. He winked at them.

"And miss all the fun?" Daniel asked.

Matthew clapped his hands together. "Now you're talking! Come on, Snake Eyes. Tell me what I'm allowed to do."

Logan filed the name *Snake Eyes* away.

"We need to find out who the cops really are," Daniel said.

"You're assuming they're not cops. Are you sure?"

"I'm sure."

"I don't know if you know this yet, Logan. But our pal Daniel here has a sniffer as powerful as a bloodhound on alien steroids. And I don't say that lightly. Daniel, I support your judgement. I will find out who these imposters are. Want me to get rid of the bodies?"

"They're probably already gone."

"What?!" Logan blurted.

"Again, I trust Daniel's judgement. If he says they're gone, they're probably gone."

"How will you find out who they are?"

"I have my ways. Don't I, Snake Eyes?"

Daniel nodded. "I hate to admit it, but Matthew has a way of finding out most anything about anyone."

"You got that right! Now, if you'll excuse me, I have work to do!"

The strange man actually skipped out of the room. When the door had closed behind him, Logan looked at Daniel and asked, "Is he really a friend of yours?"

"I wouldn't call him a friend, Logan. I'd call him a necessary evil. Now, let's get some rest. If there's one thing I know about Matthew, it's that once he starts digging, we're in for a whirlwind of an adventure."

CHAPTER 15

MATTHEW WILCOX

"I'm so excited! And I just can't hide it!" Matthew Wilcox sang to himself as he strolled down the empty sidewalk, occasionally doing a spin or a twirl.

I knew coming to New York was a good call, he thought to himself. *I wonder if I could entice Cal to join us? Nah. This'll be more fun.*

He didn't need directions to Logan's apartment. He didn't take a circuitous route. He didn't worry about being followed.

His only precaution came when he entered Logan's building. He didn't need to be seen. He went in the front, after he'd made sure that the small lobby was empty.

Then he took the stairs up to the fifth floor, peeked down the hall, and walked to Logan's apartment.

"At least they locked the door on their way out," Wilcox murmured as he slid the key Daniel had given him into the slot. This was his second time in the apartment that night. The first had been right after Daniel and Logan rushed out, right after he, Matthew Wilcox, the assassin's assassin, had shot the two fake cops from across the street, through the window, and into the now rigor-induced bodies.

"Good to see you again, old boys," Wilcox said to the bodies. Since he'd already collected their phones, wallets, and keys, the only thing left to do was wait. He was gazing out the window when the knock came.

"Come in!" he said.

Four men entered, all looking grim. Two had rolls of plastic under their arms.

"You want us to clean up the blood, too?" the lead man asked.

"Do you have the time?" Wilcox asked.

"As long as you have the money." The man grinned. He was missing one of his front teeth.

"You know I'm good for it, Jimbo. Now giddy up. I've got work to do."

As the disposal team went about their business, Wilcox checked in electronically with his forensic contractor.

Update?

No ID yet. Definitely not cops.

That was good, at least about them not being cops. Not that Wilcox held any moral high ground for killing crooked cops. But real cops left trails.

When the disposal team announced they were finished, Wilcox glanced at his watch.

"Forty-nine minutes, Jimbo. You're slipping."

Jimbo wiped the sweat from his pockmarked forehead. "Next time, call FedEx if you want it done faster."

Wilcox reached into his coat pocket and pulled out a roll of bills. "Until next time, fellas."

Jimbo caught the roll when Wilcox tossed it to him and said, "Always a pleasure. Call us again soon."

"It will be very soon, I promise."

Wilcox waved as they carried the wrapped bodies out the door. The funny thing about New York was that it was very unlikely that a) anyone would ask about the packages, and b) anyone would really even care. This was New York City, home to all manner of strange late-night activities. Besides, the disposal team looked like movers, not thugs. They even had matching uniforms to prove it.

He locked the door and took his time inspecting the apartment. Content with the job Jimbo and his men had done, Wilcox went to Logan's bedroom and tapped into the laptop on the nightstand with a special extraction device. It took three minutes. He'd peruse the information later.

The books next to the laptop and the corkboard on the wall meant nothing. Just the workings of a junior reporter trying to make it in the big city. So how had Logan Whitaker gotten caught up in someone's web?

Wilcox's phone buzzed, and he looked at the screen.

Positive ID. You want me to send it over?

Sure. Email it.

He didn't figure there was much of a rush. Whoever was behind this scheme wasn't going anywhere. And Wilcox knew that once the puppeteer lost contact with two of his/her puppets, new insights and tells would make themselves known. How and when they surfaced would inform Wilcox of the professional skill of his opponent. But more importantly, it would give him a better idea of how high his body count might be. And since it was almost Christmas, Wilcox wanted a high body count. He wanted it very much.

CHAPTER 16

IAN FITZGERALD

Ian Fitzgerald tried the number again. For the fifth time, it went to voicemail. He did not leave a message.

His watch said 7:47am. He had to meet Gregory Worthington at 8:30 for a first introduction. The seduction had worked. Good ol' Gregory would open up his Rolodex because he knew what it meant for his empire. Best to temper that excitement for a time. No need to rush things.

Ian guzzled the rest of his lukewarm coffee and picked up the phone.

That his fixer wasn't answering his phone didn't concern Ian, but it definitely annoyed him. The last he'd been told, they were on their way to have a chat with the nosy reporter, Logan Whitaker. The fixer was a competent man, a reliable employee. He kept to timelines, and his reports were brief and precise.

Ian had met the fixer at, of all places, his son's soccer game. Little Terry Fitzgerald lived with his mother in New Jersey, where his head was no doubt being filled with garbage by Ian's ex and her pain-in-the-ass family of crabby aunts, drunk uncles and cronish grandmothers. Terry was ten and uncoordinated. He spent most of his time talking to another kid on the team, a boy equally unenthused with the game. When Ian heard the man sitting next to him grumble about his kid talking to Terry, Ian figured out he was the other kid's father. The two men paid less attention to the game, and more time commiserating the fact that youth athletics had gone to hell, and their boys were on the receiving end of the emasculation of the male race.

The man had introduced himself as John. Just John.

For the next game, John brought whiskey disguised in Coke cans. He handed one to Ian. "Thought we might as well enjoy the shitshow," he'd said.

That's how they'd spent a fall, two divorcees trying to create the appearance of being good fathers.

It was on their fourth whiskey-laced hang that Ian finally asked John what he did for a living.

"Investigations," John said.

"You a cop?"

"I was for a few years. Got tired of the politics and the water cooler bitchfests. Went out on my own. Glad I did."

By the look of the man's clothes and his tone, Ian could tell that the man's business, while alive, was probably on life support.

"You ever do any work for newspapers, media outlets?" Ian had asked.

"Not really. Can't stand those SOBs."

That made Ian laugh.

During the next game, right after a meathead of a kid pushed his son down, Ian made John an offer. "How would you like to work for me?"

"I don't even know what you do."

"My business provides sources for reporters."

John made a face. "Sounds terrible."

Ian did not take offense. John's comment actually bolstered his intent.

"Sometimes we have problems. A source gets cocky and thinks they can take advantage of one of our high-paying clients."

John turned and looked at him. "You need a thug." Ian didn't reply. John shrugged. "I'd be interested in talking."

Ian had looked into John's business and knew the man was debt deep.

Two meetings later, John agreed to his first contract job for Fitzgerald & Muse. Six months later, Ian was so happy with John's performance that he convinced Gregory Worthington to pay off the man's debt and hire John full time. The investment paid off handsomely.

Now John wasn't answering his phone. They had agreed upon contingencies. If John and his team got in trouble, they'd go dark. It'd only happened once in the last three years. And that had been a misunderstanding.

Ian tried to call his fixer again. It went straight to voicemail this time.

He'd deal with it after the meeting. Ian Fitzgerald had his second billionaire to sell. With Gregory's help, Ian knew that his company would soon overflow with working capital, and his power would rise in rapid succession.

CHAPTER 17

LOGAN WHITAKER

Logan padded to the kitchen, rubbing his eyes with a yawn.

"Good morning," Daniel said. He was sitting at the massive kitchen island. There was an empty plate in front of him, and Logan thought he smelled bacon.

"Would it be rude if I made breakfast?" Logan asked.

"Too late. I already made you some. Look in the oven."

Logan walked to the commercial grade oven and open the door. There was a plate of bacon, eggs, and toast waiting for him.

"Thanks," Logan said, taking a seat at the island and digging in.

Daniel poured him a cup of coffee and brought a bottle of orange juice from the fridge.

"How'd you sleep?"

"Like the… I was going to say dead."

"You can still say it."

"I guess it doesn't change what happened last night," Logan said.

"It doesn't. Logan, there's something I want to discuss. The man I introduced you to last night."

"Matthew."

"That's right. I think it's only fair that I tell you what he is."

"*What* he is or *who* he is?" Logan asked.

"*What* he is."

"By the way you said that, I feel like I should hold on to something before you tell me."

"Maybe you should."

Logan shifted to face Daniel fully. "It's okay. If I didn't faint last night, I'm probably not going to faint now. *What* is Matthew?"

"He's an assassin," Daniel said, like he was telling Logan that Matthew was a mailman. Logan waited for a smirk, a smile or "I'm just kidding. He's a boat captain."

"You're not kidding," Logan said, finally.

"I'm not."

"And *why* did you call an assassin to help us?"

"It's complicated. That's why I thought you should know."

Logan put down the orange juice. "Were you not going to tell me?"

"It all depended on how you looked this morning."

"The fact that I didn't look like I was going to run for California made you tell me the truth?"

Daniel shrugged. "I always tell the truth, Logan. It just depends on how much of the truth a person can handle."

Logan exhaled and went back to his food. "Since we got that over with, tell me why we need an assassin to help us?"

"It's like I said last night; Matthew can find anyone."

"And kill them," Logan furnished.

"Sometimes."

"How do I know he won't kill me?"

"Because I won't let him."

Logan laughed. "I'm not sure that makes me feel better. What is it about you that's going to stop an assassin from killing me?"

Daniel's next words cut straight to Logan's brain center. "Because I'm better than him."

Logan understood the subtleties of the English language, the intonations of a person's speech. High school and college debate taught him that. Sprinkle on a degree in journalism and six months at *The Continental Ledger*, and Logan was very good at understanding the deeper meaning of word selection. Daniel didn't mean he was a better man than Matthew. He meant he had better skills than Matthew.

"You're an assassin too."

At first, Daniel didn't answer. And for a long moment, Logan thought his life was about to end. Not because of the way Daniel looked. Because of Logan's own choice of words.

"I've killed people, but I wouldn't say I'm an assassin."

"But you kill people. Regularly?"

"I'm one of the good guys, Logan."

"You'll have to excuse me, Daniel. I just woke up. I'm having a hard time processing the fact that I'm now in league with not one, but two killers. That's a helluva way to spend a snowy morning in New York City before Christmas."

"You're right. It's a lot to process. What I can tell you is that I was a Marine sniper in my past life. I was very good at my job. When I got out, I did some things; things I probably shouldn't tell you about. Now I work for a group that helps America right what's wrong in the world."

"Great. I've teamed up with a cowboy and an assassin. Sounds like a Tarantino movie."

"I'll give you time to think about it. We can find a place for you to hide until Matthew and I sort this out. If that's what you want."

It was all too much for Logan to process.

"How much time do I have to decide?"

Daniel glanced at his watch. "Thirteen minutes."

"Thirteen minutes? How did you come up with that number?"

"Matthew will be here in thirteen minutes. And before he gets here, I need to know whether you're in or out."

"Why?"

"If you're out, I need to get you away from Matthew. I don't trust him."

"What?! You're inviting an assassin back here again and you don't trust him?!"

"I told you I can handle Matthew," Daniel said calmly.

"And if I'm in? Then what? I sign a waiver saying I'm okay with either of you killing me?"

"No. If you're in, you get to help us decide what to do with the information Matthew found about Officer Francisco and his friend."

"Oh. So he found something."

"Matthew says he knows who they are and who they're working for. That's why he's coming."

Logan knew the right answer. He should hide until this was over. That was the smart play, the genius move.

But the reporter in Logan needed the truth. And he wanted to be a part of finding and exposing whoever was behind the killing of Niles Petersen and the two fake cops. He told himself that he wasn't like Matthew and Daniel, that he would only take up arms against another if his own life was at stake. Otherwise, he would stick to the journalist code and do like his boss, the great Fiona Graves. He'd keep digging until he found the answers. Danger be damned.

"Fine. I'll stay," Logan said. "But I've got one question before he gets here."

"What's that?"

"Can you make some more bacon? For some reason, I'm starving."

CHAPTER 18

DANIEL BRIGGS

"I'm surprised the kid is still here," Matthew Wilcox said when he strolled into the living room.

"We need his help," Daniel said.

"Do we? I've always believed that a reporter is a liability. They want the truth and nothing but, so help them God. And they'll keep digging until they find it."

"Sounds like you're afraid of me finding the truth," Logan said.

Wilcox's eyes narrowed and Daniel felt himself coil.

"I'm an open book, kid," Wilcox said.

"Okay. Why don't we start with how many people you've killed?"

"Logan," Daniel said. "Now's not the time."

Wilcox put up a hand. "It's okay. I see you told the snot-nosed pimp of paper pleasantries what I do for a living. That's just fine and dandy. Tell me paper pimp, you want me to tell you about each one, because I have a splendid memory, or do you want me to give you the number and nothing but? I kinda wanna see what my lurid details do to your delicate tummy."

"Enough," Daniel said. "What did you find out about the cops?"

Wilcox didn't take his eyes off Logan. Logan was trying his best to stand up to the gaze, but Daniel saw the young man's legs shaking.

"Jonathan James Pilson, aka Officer Francisco. Late of Hoboken, New Jersey. Divorced. Has one kid, a boy named Francis. Who names their kid Francis? Poor bastard. Probably grow up to be an accountant. Mr. Pilson served on the Hoboken P.D. for five years, then he struck out on his own. Started a tiny private investigation firm. Mostly filmed spouses doing dirty deeds. His dead pal, Peter Glen Mostoff, also formerly of the Hoboken P.D. Never married. No kids. Lived in an apartment with a goldfish and an overdue electric bill. Just the muscle who drove Mr. Pilson wherever he needed to go. I suggest we ransack their apartments and steal all their Pokemon cards."

Wilcox was still staring at Logan. Daniel wasn't sure if he'd even blinked.

"Matthew, eyes over here."

"The boy wonder and I are having a staring contest, Daniel. Can't you see that? Wanna give up yet, newsie? Crapped your pants yet?"

"No," Logan said, but the strain in his voice was obvious.

"Good. Cuz I can do this all day."

Daniel stood up and stepped between them. Wilcox tried to crane his neck to reconnect eye contact.

"Hey. No fair. I was gonna win," Wilcox said.

"Pilson. Who did he work for?"

"I'm not telling until paperboy says Uncle."

Daniel took a step towards the assassin.

"Now's not the time."

Wilcox looked up at him. "Jeez. Can't a guy have a little fun? You and Cal are too serious. How many times do I have to tell you to take an improv class? It'll change your life and the lives of everyone around you. Seriously. I'll even pay."

"Pilson," Daniel said.

Wilcox huffed. "Fine. Pilson works… sorry *worked,* for a firm called Fitzgerald & Muse. They're some kind of—"

"Hey! They're the guys I told you about," Logan said.

"Ahh. Come on. You're ruining my story."

"Sorry. Go ahead."

Wilcox rolled his eyes. "I was going to say that Pilson and his pal worked for Fitzgerald & Muse."

"You already said that," Daniel said after waiting for Wilcox to continue.

"Yeah, I know. But what if I had more to say? You really should have better manners, newsman."

"And what did Pilson do for Fitzgerald & Muse?" Daniel asked.

"I don't know yet. He's listed as a security consultant on their rolls. Same as his partner, though Mostoff is listed as a contractor, not employee."

"Why would a source acquisition firm need a security consultant?" Logan asked.

"What the hell is source acquisition?" Wilcox asked.

"They provide sources for media outlets, for stories and articles."

"So they feed the devil."

"If that's how you prefer to see it," Logan said. "You didn't answer my question. Why would they need a security consultant on the payroll? When I talked to Mr. Muse, he made it sound like all they did was make introductions."

"Everybody's got a security consultant these days, kid. In this guy's case, he probably gets paid to clean up the mess. You were Fitzgerald & Muse's mess." Logan gulped. "Now

I've got your attention. Don't enjoy hearing that maybe, just maybe, you were gonna get shot instead or in addition to Pilson?"

"But who killed Pilson and his buddy?" Logan asked.

"That's the magic question," Wilcox said. "My money is on Fitzgerald and his pal Muse. I say we bust in there, bounce their heads around, drink all their booze, and see if they know who killed JFK." Wilcox made a face. "Sorry, Snake Eyes. I forgot you don't drink anymore."

Daniel ignored the comment and said, "We won't knock anyone's head around, Logan."

"Ah, come on!" Wilcox whined.

"Is it okay if I offer an idea?" Logan asked.

Daniel nodded.

"I agree with Matthew. What if Fitzgerald & Muse are covering their tracks? Pilson screwed up, didn't take care of me after the Petersen killing, and the firm decided their security consultant needed purging."

"I don't know," Daniel said. "Seems soon and messy. Why not give Pilson time to interrogate you?"

"Yeah," Wilcox interrupted. "If it were me, I'd take you to a cold basement and beat you into submission. Sound about right, Snake Eyes?"

"Don't listen to him. Logan. Can you think of anything that Muse told you, how he acted, that would give you a clue to them being behind Pilson's murder?"

"No. I don't think he's the guy. Maybe it's Fitzgerald?"

"There you go, paperboy!" Wilcox hooted. He hopped off of the couch. "Let's snatch Fitzgerald, take him for a visit to my basement, and see what he has to say."

"How about we watch and listen instead?" Daniel offered calmly.

Wilcox groaned. "That sounds boring."

"And Logan, I think you should go back to work and see

what you can find out about Jimmy Mason. Maybe ask your boss about Fitzgerald & Muse."

"I can do that. But will you—"

"I'll be nearby. I promise."

CHAPTER 19

IAN FITZGERALD

"Finish your breakfast, Fitzy. You look giddy as a schoolgirl." Gregory Worthing sipped his drink delicately. Ian wondered what Good ol' Gregory's fancy club would do if he punched Good ol' Gregory in the face.

Ian stabbed a piece of lamb and forced himself to eat it. He hated lamb, but Good ol' Gregory ordered for the table.

"Do you think he'll go for it?" Ian asked, gulping down his mimosa to cover the taste of the lamb.

"Wasn't it obvious?"

No, you smug bastard. That's why I asked! Ian thought.

"I have yet to master the subtle art of billionaire tells, Gregory. Enlighten me, would you?"

"I'd be happy to. What you have to understand about Langston is that he very much wants to be like his father. Yes, the family is still worth what most would consider a large sum. But few people know that Langston's recent forays into larger and larger real estate speculations have put them on the wrong side of debt with regional lenders. If you can get him the information he requested, it would tip the scales in his direction, possibly righting the ship."

Ian knew all this, but he accepted the diatribe as one of many necessities in his relationship with Worthington.

"You didn't say how you knew he would accept my proposal."

"It was all in the way he hesitated. I know you're not accustomed to such things, but a man of worth has a certain duty to stoicism. Langston wants to be Marcus Aurelius reborn."

"Gregory," Ian said slowly. "So I know for next time, what was his tell?"

Gregory waved the question away. "You're not ready. Besides, I'll be with you to decipher the code of my people. Another mimosa?"

"No. Thank you. I've got loose ends to tie up."

"That sounds titillating."

Ian wondered if there was a class rich heirs took once they reached a certain age to make them sound as condescending as Gregory sounded now. He hadn't talked that way in school.

"It's not that interesting," Ian said. "But I have to run." He stood up from the table while Gregory remained seated. "Same time tomorrow?"

"Same time tomorrow," Gregory said, sounding bored.

Ian left his friend, who'd beckoned the maitre'd over and was giving him an earful. Ian's car was waiting, and the valet held his door open. This wasn't Ian's first time at Gregory's club, so he did not offer a handsome tip. He remembered the time he tried, the look of disappointment on Gregory's face and then, "Thank you, sir, but we don't accept tips at The Piedmont," from the valet.

Ian thanked the valet, closed the door, and called Pilson. Again, it went to voicemail. He'd give the man until the end of the day, then he'd go looking.

Until then, he had work to do. Marty Muse was going to have to get to work and do what he did best: find sources that could provide Fitzgerald & Muse's clients with what they needed. Marty didn't need to know that their client base was about to shift away from news media and into the private sector, where the pay and the power were exponential. Client support was Ian's role. And that was exactly how Ian meant to keep it.

Ian drove all the way back to the city, imagining the elbows with which he would soon be rubbing. Billionaires. Heads of state. Celebrities.

Maybe he'd marry a movie star. Maybe he'd vacation with Richard Branson.

As Ian saw it, and had since his epiphany, the sky was the limit.

CHAPTER 20

LOGAN WHITAKER

Logan almost made it to his cubicle without being seen.

"Whitaker!" Vernon's voice cut through the intern chatter.

"He's got it out for you, Logan," he heard someone whisper.

"Yeah, he was telling everyone that he's going to nail you to the wall," someone else said, followed by a round of giggles and muffled guffaws.

"Grow up," Logan said, dumping his bag on his chair and straightening his tie. If he could go toe-to-toe with an assassin, he sure as hell could take a tongue lashing from Vernon Haskins.

The first thing Logan noticed was the state of Vernon's desk. It was a mess. So was Vernon. His tie was askew and his eyes were bloodshot.

"Where the hell have you been?" Vernon said, pointing a finger at Logan.

"Running down leads."

"Leads for what?"

Logan picked a story out of the many he was researching for Mr. Pulitzer.

"The Ursula Trang case," he said.

"That's a dead end."

Logan wondered how, considering Ursula Trang had just gone on social media and implicated herself in the very scheme she been under indictment for over the last two years.

"This is yours," Vernon said, motioning to a pile of folders.

"But I've got the border story to finish, too."

"That's dead too."

"What?!"

Vernon's bloodshot eyes narrowed.

"Are you questioning me? I could have you thrown out of here in a second."

"No, it's just that, with the confirmation from Niles Petersen I thought—"

"It's dead. Get over it."

Logan grabbed the stack of folders. "Is there anything else you need?"

"Coffee. No! Espresso. A triple. And don't leave this building until you're done with those files. I need tight summaries by midnight."

"Yes, sir."

When he set the folders on his own desk, Logan sat down heavily and exhaled. How the hell was he going to look into Jimmy Mason when he had all this work to do? Sure, his life might be on the line, but wouldn't he still need a job if he kept his life?

He rushed to make a triple espresso for Vernon, who didn't look up from his furious typing to acknowledge the delivery. Then Logan went back to his desk, opened his laptop, and gave himself ten minutes to find the spot where he'd left off looking for Jimmy Mason.

Jimmy's given name was actually Jimmy, not James. He'd lived in the same apartment for six years. Logan had to go to LinkedIn to find that Jimmy was employed by the Federal Department of Corrections as some sort of consultant. Before that, Jimmy Mason graduated from Oklahoma State University, did a stint in the Army as a Military Policeman, worked for the Oklahoma State Police, then got his federal job six years before. There was no picture of Jimmy Mason. Though far from rare, it was odd. The rest of the profile was complete and up to date. Why no picture?

Logan typed in Mason's address and pulled up the street view. He was no expert in New York real estate, but the location looked expensive. Not a hundred millionaire expensive, but too expensive for someone employed by the federal government.

Ten minutes was up. He made mental notes to 1) check to see if Mason came from money, 2) investigate whether Mason owned his place, and 3) see if he could access Mason's tax returns. For now, he had to get to Vernon's summaries.

Logan looked up four hours later, eyes blurry, fingers tingling, and a groaning stomach. It was just past 2pm, and he was barely halfway through Vernon's homework assignment. He thought about pawning it off on an intern, but he knew word would get back to Vernon. Mr. Pulitzer prided himself on his "training program," which meant that anyone who worked for him did all scut work until Vernon said they no longer had to do scut work.

"It'll make you a better reporter…some day," he'd said in Logan's welcome interview.

His cell phone dinged. It was his roommate.

I forgot about Sam!

Need to talk. It's important.

Logan typed in a hasty reply.

Kind of swamped right now. Can it wait?

NO IT CAN'T!

Logan slunk down in his chair and called Sam.

"One of our neighbors called. They said there were people in our apartment, Logan."

"I thought we told you not to use your phone."

"I haven't heard from you, Logan. Tell me what's going on. Work keeps calling and I keep ignoring them. I'm going to get fired!"

"You're not gonna get fired."

"You don't know that."

"Yes, I do. You're too good at your job, Sam. Plus, it's Christmas. Look, we're close to figuring it all out," Logan lied. "It was just a misunderstanding. The cops will not bother you." At least that last part was the truth.

"That's good. When can I come home?"

"Soon. I promise."

"How soon, Logan? I left all my stuff. I can't work without—"

"Tell me what you need. I'll bring it to you. And don't forget, I think the landlord was gonna do some work, remember?" Logan said, scrambling for any excuse to keep his roommate away from the mess in their apartment.

"You never told me that."

"Yeah, it was the plumbing. You know how the bathroom sink keeps dripping? And those spots in the living area that creak? He was going to replace the floorboards, I think."

"He better give us a break on the rent if we have to be out of the apartment for that stuff," Sam said. Logan was a penny pincher by necessity, but Sam was a miser because he liked it.

"Sure. I'll ask. Hey, I've gotta go, Sam. Vernon's calling."

Sam knew all about Vernon.

"Okay. I'll text you what I need from the apartment."

"Yeah. Great. Don't forget to turn off your phone. Bye, Sam."

"Bye Lo—"

Logan hung up the phone and closed his eyes. How the hell was he going to keep all these plates spinning? Adrenaline and caffeine, he decided, and got back to work.

CHAPTER 21

IAN FITZGERALD

Ian's internal panic button had been pressed. Pilson had disappeared. It was time to find out why.

Pilson's last known location was Logan Whitaker's apartment. Ian had confirmed the location with the company's cell phone records. But when he tried to ping the phone to get a current location, it didn't work.

He drummed his fingers on his desk. Normally, he'd have Pilson sitting here giving him ideas on how to deal with the situation. Ian did not have the training or experience in stakeouts, infiltration, or physical coercion. Pilson did. But the last five years working with Pilson opened Fitzgerald's eyes to a world he'd only seen in movies. Underground grey economies and intelligence sources existed. And most times, they existed right under the noses of everyday American life.

For Ian, it became a game. It started slow. He paid the money, gave the orders, and Pilson carried out the dirty work. Ian never saw the terrified looks and blood-soaked shoes. He kept his nose clean by staying far away from the violence.

Now, he couldn't.

Ian pulled out a card from a drawer and dialed the number. It was a card Pilson gave him. "Use it if anything happens to me," he'd said.

"What could happen to you?" Ian had asked.

Pilson chuckled. "Nothing. But just in case..."

This was the just in case.

A gruff male voice answered.

"Yeah?"

"I got your number from Pilson."

"Okay."

"I can't find him."

"You've got my attention."

"I know where he was last seen. I was hoping you could look into it."

"You have a pen and paper?" the man asked.

"Yes."

"Here's the wiring information." The man rattled off some numbers, which Ian scribbled onto a pad. "Deposit of twenty thousand. My fee starts as soon as I hang up the phone."

Ian didn't like the open-ended nature of this new relationship, but he didn't have a choice. Ian thought that if Pilson was found, he could make him pay the bill.

"I understand," Ian said.

"Good. As soon as I get confirmation, I'll head to the apartment."

"I'll send it now."

The line went dead, and Ian hurried to set up the wire transfer from one of the Caribbean banks Marty Muse didn't know about.

After confirming the transfer, Ian sat back in his chair and exhaled. Maybe now he could get some actual work done.

MATTHEW WILCOX

Matthew Wilcox smiled. He'd listened in on not one, but two phone conversations today. The one between Sam and Logan. Then, the Fitzgerald guy and whatever goon was about to head Wilcox's way.

The assassin rubbed his hands together and looked out the window. Dark clouds continued to dump inches of snow on the city. The apartment heater worked overtime to keep the place warm. Wilcox wondered what Daniel was doing. Probably standing on the street watching *The Continental Ledger* building. He'd promised to stay close to Logan. And Daniel was a man of his word.

Good thing too. That kept him far away from Wilcox, who was walking to the fridge to get a snack, calculating how much time it would take for Fitzgerald's thugs to arrive. With the snow in the streets, twenty minutes at the quickest and a couple hours at the latest. Maybe they'd wait until nightfall. It didn't matter to him. Killing was killing, whether it came sooner or later.

Wilcox grabbed a jar of pickles from the fridge, twisted the lid off, and grabbed a spear.

"Sustenance," he said, thinking about the rules for this particular game. It was all a game to the assassin. He had more money than he could ever spend. What he craved was excitement and challenge. And in his experience, being close to Daniel Briggs or Cal Stokes brought more and better excitement than Wilcox could ever dream up alone. That's why the two Marines were off his personal kill list for now. Sure, he'd make their lives miserable from time to time, screw with their serenity, but death meant the end of fun. And Matthew Wilcox was all about fun.

Logan Whitaker was another story. He wasn't a bad kid, but he was a reporter. And Wilcox hated reporters, news anchors, pundits, politicians... basically anyone and anything that tried to twist the minds of those who did not know how to think for themselves. Wilcox would never consider himself a moral man. He did not live by a moral code. But when things annoyed him, like the former President of Russia who'd repeatedly annoyed him, Wilcox removed the annoyance and went on his merry way.

The question now was, who was the bigger annoyance? Logan Whitaker or Ian Fitzgerald?

Wilcox ate one more pickle, screwed the lid back on the jar, replaced it in the fridge, then washed his hands. By the time he was drying his hands, he'd decided that until he found out more about Fitzgerald, he'd let Logan live. Maybe Daniel would convince the kid to make a career change and Logan would scratch himself off Wilcox's annoyance list.

Either way, it didn't matter to Wilcox. What mattered now were the goons coming to visit. Wilcox planned on giving them a fitting surprise. Because goons were goons, and Wilcox was Wilcox.

CHAPTER 22

LOGAN WHITAKER'S APARTMENT

The man knocked on the door. No answer. No nosy neighbors poked their heads out of their respective doors, either. He knocked again. Still no answer.

"You pick the lock. I'll watch the hall," he said.

The man Ian Fitzgerald had called leaned against the carpet cleaning machine and kept a casual eye up and down the hall. When his partner clicked the last tumbler, they pushed inside.

They found a guy sprawled out on the couch. He was bare chested. His right hand rested inside the front of his jeans. And there were Cheetos all over the drool covered pillow next to the man's head.

"Look at this guy," Goon #2 said.

"Shut up. Tie him up. Gag him too."

Goon #1 pulled the pistol from his pocket and covered his partner. The man on the couch stirred. His eyes fluttered open, and he said groggily, "Hey, are you the pizza guys?"

"You Whitaker?" Goon #1 asked.

"Yeah, why?"

The pistol came up. "Hands where I can see them. Both of them."

The guy's eyes went wide. "But I'm busy down there," he said, his eyes flicking to his crotch.

"I said, put your hands—"

Too fast, the man's hand came out of his pants with something that shouldn't have been there. It took Goon #1 a split second too long to realize it was a gun. The suppressed weapon, a silenced .22 if his mind told him right, spat two times. Brain matter and blood exploded into Goon #1's face and he stumbled back. Trying to wipe his partner's insides from his eyes, he was too slow to react, and he fell over backwards. When he could finally see, he was on his back, looking up at the bare-chested man. He noted the pockmarks and scars on the man's body. Bullet and stab wounds, he thought.

"You sure you don't have any pizza?" the guy with the gun asked.

"What?"

The man shot him in the forearm connected to the hand that now flinched and dropped the pistol.

"I said, you sure you don't have any pizza?"

"No, I don't have any pizza."

"Too bad. I'm starving. You should see what they keep in their fridge. Pickles and stale beer. Kids. Am I right?"

The slightly elongated barrel pointed at the head of Goon #1. He had no doubt that the stranger would use it. He glanced over at his partner. One eye was gone, just a dark hole weeping blood. The other stared at him, lifeless and fixed.

"What do you want?" Goon #1 asked.

"I told you. I want pizza."

The man just stood there and stared down at him.

This guy is nuts, Goon #1 thought.

"Okay. I can get you some pizza," he said. Maybe playing along with crazy would work.

"Now we're talking!" the man said, yanking the goon to his feet.

He took his chance. Pretending like he was stumbling, Goon #1 wrapped his good arm around the man and yanked with all his might to flip him to the left. He was a powerful man who'd knocked his share of skulls in his lifetime. He knew how to down a man. Besides, he had to outweigh the crazy guy two times over, at least.

But instead of going down, the man with the gun somehow reversed the move, used Goon #1's momentum against him, and flipped him over the small coffee table and onto the couch.

"Naughty, naughty," said the man. He stepped up onto the couch and straddled the goon, one foot on each side of his torso. "You said you were gonna get me pizza. You lied."

"Listen, you crazy asshole, I'll buy you a thousand pizzas if it means—"

"Uh uh. This is not a negotiation. You came uninvited. What will I tell the landlord when he sees your buddy's brains on the floor and your balls sitting next to them?" The pistol's direction shifted to the goon's midsection.

"No, please."

"No, please what?"

The goon hesitated.

"Wrong answer," the man standing over him said. He pressed the trigger, and the round tore into the goon's good arm. "Shhh! If you scream, I will shoot you in the balls. If you don't, I might let you go."

The goon didn't believe the man, but what choice did he have? He bit the inside of his cheek but could do nothing about the tears of pain.

"There, there," the crazy man said. "No need to cry. Come on. Sit up. Let's have a chat." The man hopped off the couch with animal grace and sat down on the coffee table. With enormous effort, the enforcer used his under-used core to right himself into a seated position. Sweat covered his body, and blood ran down both arms.

"What do you want to know?" he asked.

"Now, why couldn't we have started with that? Everyone tries to be the tough guy. And sorry about your buddy. Looks like he could've been your brother."

"He's a cousin," Goon #1 said, wincing.

"*Was* a cousin," the man corrected. "Now. Down to business. You got a phone?"

"In my pocket."

"Good. So you don't think I'm getting frisky, I'm going to get your phone. Is that okay?"

"Do I have a choice?"

The man grinned. "You always have a choice. Didn't they teach you that in the Bronx School For Bad Boys? That's where you're from, right?" The goon froze. "I know everything about you, Alberto "The Ox" Moretti. I know you've been divorced three times. I know you have a daughter who attends Cornell. I know you just bought a used 1979 Lincoln from your Uncle Bruno."

"You been following me?"

"Let's get one thing straight. I don't give a damn about you." The man pressed the barrel to Moretti's temple. "What I give a damn about is pizza."

"You're nuts."

"Maybe. What's it to you?"

"Why don't you just kill me? I'm done talking to you."

Moretti was ready to die. His arms hurt like hell and he was pretty sure his thudding heart was about to give out.

"Well, I'm not done talking to you. This is your lucky day, The Ox. Say, why do they call you The Ox?" The barrel went from Moretti's temple to his oversized belly. "Ah, right, because you look like one. I hate obvious nicknames. They're so cliche. I would've called you something funny, like Fat

Face Moretti. How's that sound? You like Fat Face Moretti?" He said the name with an Italian accent.

"Can I get some water?"

"Not before I get my pizza," the man said. Moretti thought he had the look of a boy who'd never grown up. Willy Wonka in the flesh.

"What's with you and pizza? Did your daddy never take you to Pizza Hut in the burbs?"

The man tapped Moretti on the head with his gun. "Now that's funny. I like you, Fat Face. And no, my daddy never took me to Pizza Hut. An important man like him wouldn't be caught dead in a Pizza Hut. Thanks for dredging up terrible memories, Fat Face." The man frowned like he was going to cry. "I think you hurt my feelings." A single tear ran down the loon's face. His bottom lip quivered. "Look. You made me cry." Then, the crazy grin reappeared, and the barrel returned to Moretti's temple. "Here's what's gonna happen, Fat Face. I'm pulling your phone out of your pocket. You're going to tell me who delivers the best pizza in this neighborhood. You're going to order me an extra large pepperoni. And then I'm gonna let you leave."

"You're pullin' my chain."

The man looked all around. "I see no chain to pull. Ready for me to get your phone?"

Moretti nodded.

The man slipped the phone from Moretti's pocket. "Oh, and there's one more thing I want you to do after I let you go."

Here it comes, Moretti thought. This crazy bastard is gonna shoot me in the back of the head. Fine. Be done with it. My arms hurt too much anyway.

"What?"

"Just so we're clear, I'll let you keep the twenty thousand retainer. I thought about transferring it out of your account, but I don't really need the money. I think you'll need it to pay for arm rehab." The man shook his head like he was clearing it. "I want you to pay Ian Fitzgerald a visit and deliver him a message."

"What message?"

The man leaned in and whispered in Moretti's ear. "I want you to tell Ian that I'm going to kill him."

Once Moretti was gone, Matthew Wilcox sat down on the couch and called the cleaner. Jimbo confirmed and said, depending on traffic, that he'd be there in fifteen minutes.

Wilcox put his feet up on the dead man's back and waited for his pizza. He figured he'd earned it.

CHAPTER 23

IAN FITZGERALD

"I need to see you," Moretti said over the phone.

"That's not possible," Ian Fitzgerald replied. "I have a dinner meeting."

He didn't really have a dinner meeting, but he did not want to meet Pilson's hired gun. Wiring money to the contractor was bad enough.

"Cancel the meeting."

"I can't. It's with a very important—"

"Cancel the damn meeting!"

"I will not tolerate being spoken to in this manner. If you think you're getting another penny from me—"

"They're all dead," Moretti said.

"What? Who?"

"I'd rather not say over the phone. For your sake."

That's when it sank in. The man was saying that Pilson was dead. Not that Fitzgerald cared about Pilson's life, but he thought about what his fixer's death would mean for the future.

"Fine. I'll text you a location. Meet me there in an hour," Fitzgerald said.

The call ended, and the co-founder of Fitzgerald & Muse stared at his phone. What the hell was he going to do next?

High school students, stranded when their bus ran off the snowy off-ramp and into a ditch, packed the rest stop. It made meeting inside the rest stop building impossible. Fitzgerald thought about calling Moretti to change the location.

"You Fitzgerald?" a voice said from behind him.

He turned to face a large man whose face was pale and blotchy under the yellow awning light. He was standing awkwardly, and when he shifted his weight, he winced.

"You're Moretti."

"I need to sit down." He walked over to a table, even though everyone else was under shelter from the snow. He sat down. Painfully.

"You said it was urgent. Why did—"

Moretti's coat had shifted and Fitzgerald saw the blossom of red on the man's shirt. "What happened?"

"He killed my cousin. Damn. I could use a cigarette. Got any?"

"No."

Moretti nodded. "I'm supposed to deliver a message."

"Hold on. What about Pilson?"

"Forget about Pilson. Pilson is dead."

"How do you know that? Did you see him?"

Moretti laughed. "Are you kidding? That loony toon is gonna kill my whole family if I don't tell you this before I bleed out."

"I can take you to a hospital. If you just—"

"Shut up and let me talk," Moretti said, swaying to one

side. "This guy is nuts. Totally nuts. Kept asking for pizza. Made me order it for him."

Fitzgerald did not know what Moretti was talking about.

"And Pilson?"

"I said forget about Pilson!" Some of the braver high schoolers who were standing outside turned to look. "Now listen. I'm no amateur. But this guy, he's on another level. Never seen a guy move like that. Like a jungle cat or something. Freaky. Too loose to be former military. Fast. Real fast." Fitzgerald let the man talk. "I don't know what you got yourself into, pal, but I'm done with it. Got my life and I sure ain't taking that for granted."

"A message. You said you had a message."

Moretti grimaced. "Right. Sorry. Must be the blood. I swear I passed out on the drive over. Could barely grip the steering wheel. Don't know how I made it." He licked his lips as sweat dripped from his forehead and down his nose. "The guy wanted me to tell you that you're next. He's gonna kill you and it ain't gonna be pretty."

"Why? Did he say why?"

Moretti laughed. "Hell no, he didn't say why. If I'd asked, he'd probably say it was because you like to put green peppers on your pizza." Moretti groaned when he got to his feet. "I want another fifty for getting shot and because my cousin got killed. After that, I never want you to call me again. Understand?"

Fitzgerald sat frozen. Who wanted to kill him? And why?

"I said, you understand?" Moretti repeated.

"Yes, I understand."

Moretti nodded and started to walk away. Then he turned and said, "Consider this my last piece of advice. Run for the hills, Mr. Fitzgerald. You want none of what's comin' your way."

Ian Fitzgerald did not leave for another ten minutes. His jelly legs wouldn't let him. When he finally got up to walk to his car, Pilson's voice spoke in his head. Something he'd said when they'd hunkered down during their first life or death deal: "Go back to the beginning. Always go back to the beginning."

By the time he got to the car, Fitzgerald knew what that beginning was and where he would start: Logan Whitaker.

CHAPTER 24

LOGAN WHITAKER

It was 11:15pm when Logan pressed PRINT. The summaries were done, and he was exhausted. As he walked to the printer room, he checked his messages. Daniel said he was nearby if needed. They'd talked twice. Daniel said there was no change and no word from Matthew, the assassin.

Logan waved to a cute intern who'd asked him out once, then ducked into the printer room. Empty. *Thank the trees and the bees,* he thought, something his mother would say at bedtime when he was a boy. Logan wondered what his mother would think of his late night escapades now. Back then it was hiding under the covers, reading old editions of *The New York Post*. Now it was hanging on to work by a thread and consorting with killers.

He checked to make sure all the summaries had printed. Satisfied, he made a beeline to Vernon's office. The reporter looked worse than before. There were two half-eaten sandwiches on top of scattered handwritten notes on his desk.

Vernon's hair stuck out in every direction like he'd been pulling at it in frustration.

Logan knew the man liked to run on tight procrastinated timelines, but this show was something new.

"I have your summaries," Logan said by way of announcing his presence when Vernon didn't notice him.

Vernon looked up. His eyes were bloodshot and wild.

"You're late," Vernon said.

"It's not even 11:30. You said by midnight."

Vernon looked like he was going to argue, but went back to his computer instead. "Put them over there." He pointed to a side table.

"Do you need anything else?"

"No."

Vernon's fingers mashed the keyboard, and Logan took that as his cue to leave. As he grabbed the curved handle to close the glass door, Vernon called out, "Fiona was looking for you."

"When?"

"I don't know."

There was no elaboration. That could mean Fiona was looking for Logan earlier today, or even yesterday. Vernon had a skewed sense of time at best.

Not wanting to make her wait any longer, Logan rushed to her office. He looked through the glass as he approached and saw a man sitting in the chair across from Fiona. She perked up when she saw Logan's approach and waved for him to come in.

"You wanted to see me, Ms. Graves?"

"Have a seat, Logan."

Logan took a seat next to the man in the expensive suit. He looked vaguely familiar, but Logan couldn't pin a name. He also looked disturbed.

"Logan, this is Ian Fitzgerald," Fiona Graves said. "Ian, this is Logan Whitaker."

Logan offered his hand. Fitzgerald did not take it. That's when it hit him. Fitzgerald. As in Fitzgerald & Muse! He pulled his hand back.

"It's a pleasure to meet you, Mr. Fitzgerald. I met Mr. Muse the other day."

"You want to tell him, or should I?" Fitzgerald asked Fiona.

Logan didn't like the vibe he was getting from either. Fitzgerald hadn't looked at Logan and Fiona was acting like she didn't want to, either.

"I'll tell him," Fiona said. "Logan, Ian says you were the last person to have contact with an Officer Francisco. Do you know who that is?"

Logan thought about lying.

"Yes, ma'am."

"Would you care to tell me how you know Officer Francisco?"

How much to tell her?

"Officer Francisco was conducting an investigation."

"And how was it you got pulled into his investigation?" Fiona's eyes were the hardest he'd ever seen. He didn't want to disappoint her. Maybe she could help.

"Ms. Graves, I was tasked with verifying specific information from a source recommended by Mr. Fitzgerald's firm." Fitzgerald still hadn't turned to face him. "When I met said source—"

"It's okay for you to use his name, Logan. Mr. Fitzgerald already knows."

"Yes, ma'am," Logan said. "When I met Niles Petersen, a homeless man attacked him and stabbed him multiple times."

For the first time, Ian Fitzgerald spoke, his voice hard and condescending. "That's a lie. Niles Petersen is alive and well. I spoke to him this evening."

"It's not a lie!" Logan blurted. "It was Niles Petersen. He said so."

Finally, Fitzgerald turned to face him. "Tell me, Mr. Whitaker, how many drinks had you had that night? Or was it drugs? Mayhaps there was a cocaine pre-party before you left the office?"

Logan looked at Fiona for help. She just stared. "Ms. Graves, I've never touched a drug in my life. And no, I wasn't drunk. I'm telling the truth!"

"I don't believe you," Fitzgerald said. "Tell him, Fiona."

Fiona Graves looked uncomfortable again. "The police are on their way here, Logan."

"For what?"

"To question you."

"But I already talked to them."

"Logan, listen to me. It's very important that you understand that this is out of my hands. If you'd come to me before, then maybe—"

"Enough!" Fitzgerald boomed. "Mr. Whitaker, the police are on their way here to arrest you for the murder of Kevin Hanson, Officer Francisco and his partner, Officer Gelando."

Logan rose from the chair. "You can't do this. Ms. Graves, I swear, I had nothing to do with this. Someone's trying to frame me."

"Sit down, Logan," Fiona said.

He did not sit down. "I'm sorry, Ms. Graves, but I can't go with the cops. I don't trust them. What if—"

"This is absurd," Fitzgerald said. "I'll put you in handcuffs myself. Officer Francisco was not only an excellent police officer, he was a friend. And if you think I will stand here and let you tarnish his memory, you've got—"

Logan didn't hear the last words that came out of Fitzgerald's mouth, because his heart was thudding so hard that when he ran for the door, all he could think about was spending the rest of his life in prison.

CHAPTER 25

DANIEL BRIGGS

Daniel sat with his eyes closed, listening to the newcomer share her story. As luck would have it, he'd found an Alcoholics Anonymous group that ran meetings all day just around the corner from Logan's office. Rather than stand on the street and freeze, Daniel settled in to his home away from home and got reacquainted with the New York City style of sobriety.

"Thank you, Gina," the room of twelve attendees said together when the newcomer had finished. She sniffled into a tissue. The woman next to her leaned in and wrapped an arm around the broken thing.

That was why Daniel had once again come to love the program. No matter where he went, he found family. In every city, he had a home.

The chairperson was going through the script to end the meeting when the text from Logan came through.

> In a lot of trouble. Where are you?

Daniel rose and exited the room. He texted back quickly.

Around the corner. Headed your way.

He was outside by the time Logan texted back.

Need to get away from the office. Meet at...

Daniel waited for the rest. A pinned location came through. It was a small public park three blocks away.

Daniel made it to the park first. When Logan arrived, he was wide-eyed and panting.

"I think...they're following...me," Logan said, bending over to put his hands on his knees. His pants were wet up to his thighs, and he wasn't wearing a coat.

"Here," Daniel said, taking off his coat and draping it on Logan's shoulders. "Catch your breath. Then tell me what happened."

For a long minute the only sound in the muffled snowy night was the far off honk of a delivery truck and Logan's labored breathing.

Logan righted himself and put his arms into Daniel's coat.

"Fitzgerald. He came to the office."

"Fitzgerald. As in Fitzgerald & Muse?"

"Yeah. He wouldn't look at me. Took a minute to realize I was in trouble. I should've seen it. I'm so stupid."

"Logan, it's okay. Just tell me."

Logan nodded, took a deep breath, and told Daniel everything. When he finished, he asked, "Do you think I should go back? I don't want to go to jail. Seriously. What will my mom think?"

"You're not going to jail," Daniel said.

"How do you know that?" Panic and tears filled Logan's eyes.

"Look at me, Logan. When I tell you you're not going to jail, you're not going to jail."

"I wouldn't be so sure of that," said a voice from the shadows.

Logan spun, and Matthew Wilcox walked into the clearing.

"Where have you been?" Daniel asked.

"Doing the dirty work while you played wet nurse."

"You were supposed to be watching Fitzgerald. Instead, Fitzgerald showed up at Logan's work and accused him of murder. The authorities are involved."

Wilcox picked something from his tooth and flicked it away. "The authorities aren't involved."

"How do you know that?" Logan asked, a little too forcefully.

Daniel watched Wilcox's body language change.

"I just know," Wilcox said, his voice making it obvious that he was losing patience with explaining himself to a kid.

"Matthew, what did you find out about Fitzgerald? Why does he think Logan killed Pilson and his partner?"

"Oh, I don't know, Daniel, maybe because the last place Fitzgerald knows Pilson was is at paperboy's apartment? And maybe Logan has something to tell us. Do you, newsie? How'd Pilson's body disappear? You run a body disposal business on the side?"

"What?! No. Of course not." Logan looked at Daniel.

"Don't listen to him, Logan. In fact, don't even talk to him."

Wilcox's face softened. "Ah, come on, guys. I thought we were simpatico. Friends. Best buds 'til eternity do us part. I was just joshing with you, Logan. I don't think you made Pilson and Pilson Number Two disappear. But I do think Fitzgerald had something to do with it. Think about it. You get wise, start poking around, he figures Pilson is trash for getting it wrong. Fitzgerald wipes out the problem and pins it on you. Makes sense, right?"

"Do you have any proof?" Daniel asked.

"I'm working on some leads. Nothing concrete, yet. Next step is to have a one-on-one with Fitzgerald."

"I'll come with you," Daniel said.

"You think that's a good idea? You're one of the good guys, Daniel. What if Fitzgerald has cameras everywhere? You want your face plastered on every screen in America? That's right. I didn't think so. Let's face it. I'm expendable. Let me do what expendables do best: stir the pot and see what demons crawl out."

Wilcox wasn't wrong. He was technically expendable, though not completely trustworthy. But if what Wilcox was saying was true, that the authorities weren't after Logan, that it was a ruse orchestrated by Fitzgerald, Daniel had his own way of finding that out.

"Okay. You talk to Fitzgerald. I'll take Logan to the apartment."

"Sounds like a plan, Stan," Wilcox said. "Anyone wanna grab some shawarma before we part? I just watched *Avengers*, and it gave me a hankering for shawarma. If it's good enough for Captain America, it's good enough for me."

"We'll eat at the apartment. Thanks," Daniel said.

"Your loss. See you when I see you!"

Wilcox whistled a merry tune that sounded like a song from *Annie* as he strolled out of the park.

"He needs to be committed," Logan said when the assassin had disappeared.

"Right now, we need him."

"You sure?"

"With Matthew, you can never be one-hundred percent sure of anything."

CHAPTER 26

IAN FITZGERALD

He slept at the office because he was too afraid to go home. The office had high-tech locks and hired security. Home had a middle-aged doorman who was better at playing solitaire than keeping dangerous men out.

Ian Fitzgerald tossed and turned on the couch most of the night. He kept thinking about Pilson. His mangled face crept from the darkest corners of Ian's dreams and wept bloody tears until Ian woke up panting. It was 5am when he decided to get up, grab a cup of coffee from the lounge, and just get to work.

Ever efficient, early and chipper, Marty Muse passed by his office at exactly 6am.

"You been here all night?" Marty asked.

"What gave it away?"

"Your hair. You're wearing the same suit you wore yesterday. And you're here before eight o'clock. What's up?"

Ian yawned. "I was going to talk to you about it later this week, but since you're here..."

Marty's face drooped. It did that when he was worried.

Marty loved to worry. "Is everything okay? Is it the business? I thought we were in the black."

"Oh no. The business is fine. Just fine. In fact, we're expanding."

Ian hadn't planned on telling Marty what he was doing until much later, until they were rolling in the money and it was too late to back out. But since the universe seemed to have other plans, maybe old reliable Marty Muse could help Ian fast track his plans.

"That's a relief. I thought you were going to say we lost a client," Marty said.

"Actually, I'm about to sign our biggest client ever."

Marty perked up. "Wow! Who is it? CNN?"

"We're pivoting, Marty. We'll still provide source acquisition to our friends in the media, but corporations will pay much more for our people. This contract alone will double our annual income. And that's only for starters!"

He watched Marty mull over Ian's words. Marty was a muller. He probably mulled more than Leonardo DaVinci ever had.

"Corporations? What do they need our sources for?"

Ian had to be careful. Marty's job and expertise was to find the sources. Ian's job was to sign and cultivate the relationship between the source and the firm's clients. Basically, once the sources were in the door, Marty had very little, if anything, to do with them. That didn't mean he couldn't rock the boat if he wanted.

"They want market research. Eyes on the ground. Expert testimony. That sort of thing."

Marty nodded. Ian hoped he'd take the bait.

"So you're saying that corporations want to pay us thousands—"

"Not thousands, Marty. Millions."

"They want to pay us millions of dollars for the same thing we're doing now?"

Ian clapped his hands. "Exactly! It's like you said from the very beginning, we're the recruiters. Only we failed to see the high demand for our services. I have you to thank, Marty. Without your keen eye for talent, there's no way this could've happened."

Marty was a muller, but he was a straightforward man. Ian knew that the right words of praise propped up poor Marty as if Napoleon called a pimple-faced private from his army and asked him to be his right-hand man.

"This is very unexpected, Ian. I can't tell you how pleased I am that our little venture—"

"What have I told you, Marty? Together, it won't be a little venture for long. In fact, how would you like to give a series of lectures at NYU detailing your thoughts on source acquisition?"

As a kid, it'd been Marty Muse's dream to go to NYU. He hadn't because his parents couldn't afford it. Marty told Ian that story the night they'd toasted their new venture.

"NYU? Really? Ian, how did you—"

"Marty. You sell yourself short every single time. You deserve this."

There were no guest series of lectures at NYU… yet. If Gregory Worthington had taught Ian anything, it was that you made your own destiny, and sometimes that meant dangling the carrot before the carrot was in your possession.

"Thank you, Ian. I can't tell you how much this means to me."

Ian got up from his desk and walked over to his partner. "I know how much it means to you, Marty. Who knows, maybe this'll wake up those NYU clowns and they'll ask you to make it permanent."

Marty's eyes danced with delight. Ian thought his friend was going to cry.

"If there's anything I can do to help with the expansion, let me know," Marty said. The look on his face was priceless.

"Just keep doing what you do best, Marty. In fact," he walked back to his desk and picked up a handwritten list. "How quickly do you think you can find five sources for these?" It was a list he'd need to provide Gregory's billionaire friend, Langston, with what he needed to save his family's fortune.

Marty scanned the list.

"Sure. This should be easy."

Ian slapped him on the back. "Fantastic! I'll let the client know. Now, if you'll excuse me, I've got a mess of work to get back to." He ushered the still shocked Marty out the door.

Now that he had one set of balls rolling, he could deal with the devil at the window: whoever had scared the goon Moretti. Ian shivered when he thought about it. At least he had Pilson's contacts now. That's how he'd spent the morning, figuring out exactly which contractors he should use to get rid of Pilson's killer, and shut Logan Whitaker up for good.

CHAPTER 27

GREGORY WORTHINGTON

Gregory Worthington told his driver to stay at the curb. He wouldn't be long. Normally, he would stay in the car, but he felt that showing himself at Fitzgerald & Muse would help to keep Fitzy's ego in check. Upstarts could be such a hassle. They had a knack for screwing things up and thinking they might be emperor one day.

He'd only been to the office once, to share a celebratory glass of horrid champagne with Fitzgerald and Muse, so he didn't know the security guard at the front desk.

"Name, please," the man said, sounding as bored as he looked.

"Gregory Worthington. I'm here to see Ian Fitzgerald."

"Does Mr. Fitzgerald know you're coming?" the guard asked, as if he was reading a script.

"He does not."

"I'll have to call."

Gregory tried not to let his annoyance show. It was best to keep his calm around the peons of the world. He was to appear magnanimous, not malevolent. That was how his grandfather had put it.

"Yes, sir. I have a Mr. Worthington in the lobby," the guard said into the phone. "Yes, sir."

The guard hung up the phone and said, "Are you the same Gregory Worthington who attended Hawthorne Crest?"

Gregory tried to keep his surprise from showing.

"Yes, in fact I am. I'm sorry, do I know you?"

The guard took off his security cap. "You don't recognize me?"

"I apologize. What has it been, thirty years?"

"Thirty one, actually."

Gregory glanced at the man's name tag.

"Oscar. What is your family name?"

Maybe this apple fell very far from the family tree. You only attended Hawthorne Crest Preparatory if you came from substantial means, or if your father was a professor like Fitzy's.

"Wilde. You don't remember me? We sat next to each other our senior year. English literature."

"Oscar Wilde. Like the writer?" Gregory asked.

"Hot damn, you do remember!" The guard reached over, grabbed Gregory's hand, and shook it hard. "I'd heard you were one of the Fitzgerald & Muse owners. I never thought I'd get to see you. You're a busy man, of course. I'd hoped to see you. And now I have!"

He hadn't let go of Gregory's hand.

"It's a pleasure to see you again, Oscar, but I really must go."

He tried to pull his hand away, but the guard held on. His grip clamped uncomfortably.

"Come on, Greggy. Don't you want to relive old times? Remember the night we stripped down to our skivvies, ran through the quad lathered in baby oil, and hooted at the moon like we were Indians?"

"No, I do not. And do let go of my hand."

Oscar's eyes went wide. "Oh, your hand." He looked down like he'd just realized what he'd done. But he didn't let go. "It's such a nice hand. Right here, I remember this freckle. We named it pea pod. Remember?"

Gregory glanced at the door.

"I have to—"

The guard pulled Gregory closer so that they were both leaning over the desk. The man's breath smelled of spearmint and clove.

"I'd suggest you run on home, Greggy."

"Why is that?" he said, trying to sound casual.

He tried to yank away again but could not. He thought of yelling for help. The words stuck in his throat.

"Ian's been a bad boy. You know he killed a guy?"

"What?! That's impossible. Fitz— Mr. Fitzgerald is an upstanding—"

"Upstanding, my rear buttocks, Greggy. Now you seem like you've grown into a real fine fellow. Maybe take my suggestion and stop introducing Ian to your friends."

How could this man know?

"Who are you?"

"Someone you don't want to fuck with, Greggy. Now, because I have a lunch date, I'm going to let go of your hand. Are you going to walk back to your car, calmly, and not tell Fitzy that we met?"

"I don't even know who you are!"

The man laughed. "You will soon enough. For now, Ian's the only one I care about." He clamped down on Gregory's hand even harder. "But you're next, Greggy. You see, there are a few things I hate in this world. One: water chestnuts. They're disgusting. No flavor and a horrible texture. Two: reporters like your buddy Fitzy. And Three: billionaires with a silver spoon stuck so far up their anal orifice that they actually believe the condescending shit that comes out of their mouth. You get me, Greggy?"

"I think so."

The man released Gregory's hand.

"Good! Now run along. I've got important work to do."

The strange guard replaced his cap, adjusted it, and pointed at the exit.

Gregory Worthington didn't hesitate. When he got in the car, he ordered his driver to get the hell out of the bloody city.

MATTHEW WILCOX

Wilcox grinned as he watched Gregory Worthington hurry to his car. Now that he'd sliced the link between Fitzgerald and his benefactor, the added pressure on Fitzgerald's shoulders meant all manner of fun for the assassin. He loved to see his targets squirm. The more squirming, the better.

Now, to ramp up the pressure on everyone.

Wilcox tossed the security cap into the lap of the real security guard sitting gagged in the corner.

"Sorry for the inconvenience, friend." He put a finger to lips. "And remember, mum's the word!"

CHAPTER 28

LOGAN WHITAKER

"Bagels! Who wants bagels?!" Matthew announced as he sauntered into the penthouse after being buzzed in. "I've got lox. I've got cinnamon raisin. I've got sesame. And for you, Snake Eyes, plain on plain. Did I get that right?"

Logan looked over at Daniel, who didn't ruffle.

"Did you talk to Fitzgerald?" Daniel asked.

"Negative. Security's tight at Fitzgerald & Muse. Didn't want to risk it." He tossed Logan a wrapped bagel that felt like it weighed five pounds. "That's a sugar-crusted bagel with strawberry cream cheese. I hear you kids like all that sweet stuff. Sorry I didn't have time to stop at Starbies."

"Thanks," Logan said, not meaning it. Logan exchanged his bagel for another after he deposited the overflowing bag on the table.

"You were right about the police," Daniel said, selecting a bagel from the stack.

"Told you," the assassin said. "What, you didn't believe me?" Daniel didn't respond. "Daniel Felonious Crustaceous Briggs, how many times do I have to tell you that the secret to a long and healthy friendship is communication?" He grinned and took a hulking bite of bagel and smoked salmon.

"Tell him what you found on Mason," Daniel said.

Logan nodded. "I don't think Mason exists."

"Come again?" Matthew said through a mouth full of food.

"I couldn't find any pictures. Jimmy Mason doesn't have any social media accounts. His LinkedIn profile is stellar except for his profile picture, which is just a snapshot of some place in the woods."

"So what? The guy enjoys playing in the woods. So does Daniel."

"I think we should go see him," Logan said.

"Sure. But don't you think it'd be safer if you two stayed here? I don't want a hair on your pretty little head to get hurt. And neither do you, right, Snake Eyes?"

"Logan and I will visit Mason. You stay on Fitzgerald."

"What? This is so boring. Come on. Let's go get Mason together, then we can tie him to Fitzgerald, put a snake in their pants, and see who talks first."

"No."

"No now or no never?" Matthew asked, batting his eyes.

The two men stared at each other.

Logan said, "We don't even know if Jimmy Mason is involved. Maybe it's just a coincidence."

"You just said he had a creepy, woodsy profile picture. I think that's enough to take the guy out back and slap him around. Sounds like a real weirdo," Matthew said.

"Do you ever take things seriously?" Logan dared to ask.

The assassin stuffed the rest of his bagel into his mouth. "Not really. Life's too short. Don't they tell you that at Berkeley?"

"I went to Stanford."

"Oh! My fault. But I'm pretty sure they teach things like life lessons at Stanford, don't they?"

"Do we have to put up with this?" Logan asked Daniel.

"Don't let him get to you," Daniel said. "Matthew, I think you should visit Niles Petersen. Logan will give you the address."

"I thought that guy was a dead end… literally," Matthew said.

"There is a man posing at Niles Petersen. Talk to him. Don't hurt him. If you have to, bring him to us."

Matthew hopped to his feet. "Yes, Capitan!" He reached down and grabbed another bagel. "I have a feeling I might need this. Sustenance to put up with a weeny whose parents named him Niles. Toodle-oo, gentlemen!"

Logan watched the assassin leave, thinking that the crazy ward was where Matthew really needed to go. He looked at Daniel. "Why did you send him to see Petersen?"

"Because I have a hunch."

"Wanna let me in on it?"

"Not yet. For now, let's focus on Jimmy Mason."

Logan had learned that when Daniel wanted to explain, he would explain. Best to go along with the man's quiet confidence. Better that than the sinister bravado of the assassin who'd just left.

CHAPTER 29

MATTHEW WILCOX

If there hadn't been a foot-and-a-half of snow on the ground, he might've skipped his way down the street.

Daniel was too easy. Wilcox didn't know all the details of the sniper's recent escapades, but he knew it resulted in some sort of inner search for meaning or some such similar woo-woo. From what Wilcox had seen, that meant Daniel was being more cautious, and much more black and white.

"There is no black and white when you live in a world of gray!" Wilcox said out loud.

There was so much to do and so much time. Fitzgerald was squirming. Daniel and Logan were chasing tails. He had no doubt that they would eventually find the truth, but the truth didn't matter as much to Wilcox as the journey it took to get there.

Unlike most of the city, he didn't have a family to get to for Christmas. There were no logs on the fire, cookies baking in the oven, stockings waiting for Santa. For Wilcox, his work was his everyday gift. In his own way, he was one of the happiest people he'd ever met. He accepted anything and everything as the way it should be. Despite being captured on more than one occasion, Matthew Wilcox lived a life of freedom. He'd learned from each downturn, like he was learning now.

His first impulse was to needle his prey. Once needled, they usually twisted and turned, leading to the next adventure. He didn't put on the full court press until he saw the panic in their eyes. Then he ended the game. Then he got his ultimate satisfaction. That did not make him a sadist, at least in his mind.

When he arrived at Niles Petersen's place, a young woman with a great dane held the door so he could enter. Wilcox helped her with her umbrella while the big dog shook off the snow.

"Thank you," the woman said, taking back the umbrella.

"You are most welcome. And may I say, that's a lovely dog."

She actually blushed like she'd been the one complemented. Wilcox would never understand pet people. They'd rather live on rice and beans than give their pets anything less than the high-shelf food from the boutique pet shop down the street.

He went for the stairs as she took the elevator.

Wilcox knocked on the door of Petersen's unit. No footsteps. No scraping of chairs. He knocked again. Still no answer.

Picking the lock wasn't hard. He was inside in under a minute.

"Hello?" he called out. "Niles?"

No answer.

The place was nice, neat, and cold. The thermostat read 55 degrees.

Wilcox took a tour of the place. He agreed with Logan. The place was too nice for a guy in Petersen's line of work to afford. Was the Worthington fortune paying for the home, or was it coming from somewhere else? And what was the point? In Wilcox's experience, sources were only as good as the position they held, the money you paid them, and the gun pointed at their foreheads.

The second time around the place, Wilcox looked in drawers, under cushions, on top of cabinets.

The third time, he pulled out a small device and switched it on. He walked slowly through each room, waving the wand-like device in careful patterns. The first hit came in the kitchen, in a tablet that was supposedly powered off but propped against a knife block. The second hit came in the bedroom. The camera was inside a vintage Polaroid camera sitting on a shelf. Wilcox picked up the camera and waved. Then, he took the camera to the kitchen, set it next to the first camera in the tablet, fetched a piece of paper from the writing desk in the living room, along with a pen, wrote something down and flashed the paper at the camera. The note read: *Hi! I'm going to find you. Then, I'm going to kill you.*

He smiled wide for both video cameras then smashed them on the ground.

He put the crumbled paper in his pocket, took one last look around, and left.

It was time to make Fitzgerald talk.

CHAPTER 30

DANIEL BRIGGS

"How did you know about the cops?" Logan asked. "That they aren't looking for you?"

"Yeah."

"I have friends," Daniel said, cleaning up what was left of breakfast. Sure, he had friends with near limitless means and access, but tapping into the Stokes network wasn't something he wanted to make a habit of. Not yet.

"You know, Matthew wasn't wrong," Logan said.

"About what?"

"About communication. I give a little. You give a little…"

Daniel smiled. He genuinely liked Logan. He was young and still optimistic enough of the world to keep life fresh and exciting. Daniel wondered how this chapter in Logan's life would be written.

"There's an FBI agent I know. We help each other from time to time. He did a search and your name didn't pop up."

"How do you and this FBI agent know one another?" Logan asked.

"Like I said, we've helped each other—"

"From time to time. Yeah, I remember." Logan didn't say it snidely, like he was trying to get a rise out of Daniel. He said it like a friend; like someone who was comfortable with the back and forth.

"Look, Logan, I'll be honest with you. I'm not sure how much of my past you really want to know."

"Are you trying to keep me safe, or are you afraid I'll write a shocking exposé on the former Marine sniper who saved my life and probably did the same for a lot of other people."

"What if I say both?"

"Then I'd say that you're a smart man. I'm sorry I asked you about killing people. That was inappropriate," Logan said.

"It's okay. You wouldn't believe what people will ask you when you tell them you were in the military."

Logan laughed. "Yeah, actually I do. I had a buddy who enlisted in the Army right after high school. When he came back from boot camp, one girl we graduated with asked him how many grenades they let him bring home, and if she could throw one. Anyway, I'm sorry."

"Don't worry about it. Let's focus on Jimmy Mason. What's your gut tell you?"

Daniel watched Logan as the younger man gathered his thoughts. He was going to be an impressive journalist one day. As long as he could keep Logan alive.

"It's all a cover for something."

"Who do you think is behind it?"

"Fitzgerald, to a certain extent. Maybe Mr. Muse. Hell, the way Vernon looked, he could be in on it too."

"What about your boss, Ms. Graves?"

"I doubt it. She built her career on exposing this sort of thing."

"That doesn't mean—"

"She's a good person, Daniel."

"Good people do bad things."

"Not this one. I'd swear on a Bible that Fiona Graves is one of the most morally incorruptible people on the planet. Do you know she has almost been killed twenty times? And those are just the ones she's talked about publicly. No, I put my money on Ian Fitzgerald."

"Let's keep all options open. The bad guys have a way of making themselves known," Daniel said.

"I always wondered about that. Is it like in the movies, where the bad guy spouts off to his best friend at the bar, and that's how he gets caught?"

"Sometimes. But in my experience, it's the pressure that finally gets them to move. They make a mistake, and usually that mistake is tiny. At least with the really cagey ones."

"And that's when we pounce, right?"

"That's the plan, Logan. Now, I'm gonna go see Jimmy Mason. And you're going to dig into every Fitzgerald & Muse source you can find."

"I thought I was coming with you."

"Change of plans. I told you I had a hunch."

"And that is…?"

"Like I said, we apply pressure and the bad guys get nervous. In my experience, that means they get desperate. I don't want you exposed when that happens. That means you stay here. Understood?"

Logan nodded. "Understood."

LOGAN WHITAKER

After Daniel left, Logan did as instructed. He poured over Vernon's source list. But all he could think of was Daniel. The guy was a man of action. Logan wanted to be a man of action. Not a killer. Not a guy waving a gun around. He wanted to be like Fiona, cold and determined in her duties. And Logan knew he couldn't be that kind of journalist sitting in a fancy apartment sipping on expensive coffee. No, he needed to be out in the world, knocking on doors, talking to real people, doing what reporters of old did in their sleep: find the story and give it to the world.

Because there was a mountain of story here. He could just see the outline of the monster, but felt the image coalescing in his subconscious. Logan remembered his dad saying that his only son had a freakish talent for solving puzzles. He'd set both the Rubic's Cube and jigsaw puzzle records in his high school. Yeah, he came from that kind of town. Not only that, he was the guy everyone invited to help them break time records in popular escape rooms. To Logan, the pieces just added up.

There was one person he had to see first, someone who'd done what he was trying to do. He waited a half hour before leaving. Logan hoped Daniel wouldn't be too angry with him. But there was a story to unravel, and the journalist in Logan very much wanted to be the one who cracked the code.

He didn't see the man across the street smoking a cigarette, watching him leave. He didn't notice the man snapping photos with his phone from the Starbucks as he passed. He didn't sense the eyes of the woman tracking him as she spoke into her phone, relaying Logan's exact location to the rest of her team. Matthew's visit to Petersen's apartment had stirred up the other side.

CHAPTER 31

IAN FITZGERALD

"I'm sorry, sir, Mr. Worthington is not seeing visitors today," the machine-gun-toting guard told Fitzgerald from behind the concrete barricade leading up to Gregory Worthington's estate.

"Tell him it's Ian Fitzgerald and that it's an emergency."

"I'm sorry, sir."

Ian thought about making a run for it. The machine gun resting comfortably in the muscled man's hands convinced him otherwise.

He tried calling Gregory again. Still no answer.

Well, screw you, old chum, Ian thought, hoping his rich friend could see the middle finger he was raising in his mind.

There was plenty of room to maneuver around the driveway. A semi could've made the U-turn with ease, but Ian's late-model Mercedes struggled to gain traction on the snow. "Go, you piece of—"

The tires caught and down the driveway he slid, narrowly missing a hedgerow. He had to figure out another way to get Gregory to listen.

The car thankfully came to a stop at the bottom of the hill with inches to spare. An HVAC repair truck rumbled by on chain-covered tires when the call came through.

"Please tell me you have good news," Ian said.

"We found Logan Whitaker."

Ian put the car in park so he could concentrate. He'd seen the guy in Petersen's apartment. Was he working with Whitaker?

"Where is he?"

"Still in the city. It looks like he's headed to *The Continental Ledger*," the woman said. According to Pilson's file, she and her team were the best. They better be, considering the price tag. Ian figured it was an investment in his future which he would not see go up in flames.

"You're sure that's where he's headed?"

"Looks that way," she said.

"I know this is outside your job description, but can you grab him?"

There was a pause before the woman answered. "It'll cost you double."

"Double?"

"It's like you said, we don't do snatch and grabs."

Ian rolled his eyes. "Fine. Just make sure he gets there. And if there's a change, call me."

"You're the boss," the woman said.

Ian pressed the button to end the call. He had a decision to make. The surveillance firm promised anonymity. No one could track them back to Fitzgerald. But if he made this next call, if he brought civilians into the fray…

What choice did he have? He needed to show Gregory that he had business under control.

He made the call.

"Vernon Haskins," the reporter answered.

"Vernon. It's Ian Fitzgerald. I need a favor."

LOGAN WHITAKER

Logan made it to the office without incident. The heavy news day packed the place even though Christmas was close. No one gave him a second look when he came in, took off his coat and straightened his tie before going to see Fiona. She could help. She would know what to do.

He made it three steps out of his cubicle when an ear splitting, "Whitaker!" cut through the floor. Everyone turned, looked at him, then went back to their work.

Logan walked to Vernon's office.

"You rang?"

"Don't give me that bullshit. Get in here. And close the damn door."

Logan did as he was told, but he did not cower.

"Vernon, I have a meeting with Ms. Graves."

Vernon Haskins's appearance was a 180 from the day before. Today, he looked put together. Logan guessed he had an on-air interview later in the day.

"Pick up the phone," Vernon said, pointing at the phone on his desk.

"Sorry?"

"I said pick up the phone."

Logan picked up the receiver and held it out for Haskins.

"Put it to your ear."

Logan put the phone to his ear. He heard a dial tone.

"Now dial the following number."

Vernon recited a phone number and Logan started punching in the digits. He was halfway through before he realized what the number was.

"You want me to call the NYPD?" he asked.

"Hey! Look at the smart guy! You're finally coming

around. Tell me, smart guy, do they teach forensics at Stanford?"

"I don't know. Why?"

"Because you better've covered your tracks, cuz the NYPD is—"

Logan replaced the receiver in the cradle, noting the way his hand shook.

"Pick up the phone," Vernon said.

Logan backed away from the desk. He felt like he was going to pass out. He never should've come. He was right. Vernon was in on it.

"I have to see Fiona," he barely managed to say.

"Why? So you can hide behind her skirt? Let me tell you something, Logan, Fiona Graves can't get you out of—"

"Can't get him out of what?" Fiona's voice cut through the room like a scythe.

"Ms. Graves," Logan said. "I can explain—"

"Fiona, I wouldn't touch this kid with a ten-foot pole if I were you. Let me call the—"

"Vernon. While I appreciate your input, I believe I can handle Mr. Whitaker. Logan, go to my office."

Logan hurried out, but not before hearing, "How many times do we have to talk about how you treat—" And then he was running, because the bagels gurgled up from his stomach and he just made it to Fiona's office before vomiting in her trashcan.

He was sitting on a chair, bent over and sucking air when Fiona arrived, closing the door behind her.

"Ms. Graves, I'm sorry I—"

"Don't worry about the trashcan, Logan." She walked to the bar in the corner, clinked ice cubes into a crystal glass, poured something into the glass, walked to Logan, and handed him the drink.

"Here. You look like you need this."

The smell of whiskey almost made him heave again. He

somehow forced the liquid down, the booze warming his throat and insides. He finished the drink and looked up at his boss. He wanted to cry.

"Better?" Fiona asked.

"Yes, ma'am. Thank you."

"Get yourself some water. Then we're going to discuss exactly what you've been up to. According to Vernon, you belong in jail. By the way you responded, I surmise he might not be far from the truth." She put a hand on his shoulder. "I've been in my share of pickles, Logan. I'm sure we can figure this out together."

While he'd been sure that Fiona Graves was the person to help him before leaving the Central Park penthouse, he wasn't so sure now. He wasn't so sure of anything.

CHAPTER 32

LOGAN WHITAKER

"You've been busy," Fiona said. "Do you feel like giving up yet?"

He'd told her everything. Well, almost everything. He'd left out Daniel and Matthew. Logan did not want to get on the assassin's bad side. He had no doubt that Matthew would dispose of him in a blink.

"I want to find out who's behind the coverup."

"And tell me again why you think it's Ian Fitzgerald," Fiona said.

"He has the most to gain. Period."

"What if there's another player you don't know about? How do you account for the unknown?"

She was testing him and he knew it. He very much wanted her on his side.

"I assume there's always an unknown, and I keep pulling the string until the whole thing unravels, hopefully exposing the entire scheme."

Fiona sat back and nodded, very much looking like a college professor who approved of her student.

"And you believe the scheme is…"

"I don't know yet. Like I said, I think it has something to do with manipulating sources—"

"That's a very serious accusation, Logan. If it ever came to light that the sources our company and many others have used to corroborate stories are tainted, it would hold our entire profession up to ridicule."

"Aren't we already?" Logan asked.

"This isn't a game, Logan. I want you to find your answers, but finding the truth doesn't always mean exposing it to the world. I haven't always reported on what I've seen and heard. Sometimes the message runs through private channels. Secure channels. Channels that lead to halls of power where change can actually happen."

Logan felt like he'd been kicked in the gut. He waited for Fiona to take back the comment. "You're serious?"

"Did you think our job as journalists is so black and white that we expose the world to its own evils at every turn? Being a brilliant journalist means being discerning, understanding what can help, what can wound, and finally what can hurt and sometimes kill. Would you air a story if you knew it would lead to someone's death?"

"But we can't—"

"We can't what? Make assumptions? We make assumptions all day long, Logan. I wish the world *were* black and white. I wish the news *were* the news and nothing but. That is not the world we live in. People lie. Good men want power. Wicked men want to be forgiven. I think I understand less of the world today than I did the day I went on my first assignment."

"But, Ms. Graves, you've been to war and back, multiple times. You've looked into the face of evil and survived. Surely you have better insight now than before?"

Fiona got up from her chair and walked to the window.

"It's a big world out there, Logan. But sometimes it's the

story we write up here." She tapped a finger on the side of her head. "That's the hardest to wrap our head around." She turned to face him. Resolute. "I'll take care of Vernon. I don't think he has anything concrete."

"I'm free to go?" Logan's body released a shiver of relief.

"This is your story, Logan. Run with it. But know that there's only so much I can do to protect you. If you get caught in someone else's web, there may not be much I can do. Understood?"

Logan got up, still feeling unsure, but stronger. "I understand, Ms. Graves. Thank you for your faith in me."

"Do you have somewhere you can go? Somewhere safe?"

"Yes, ma'am."

"Good. If I were you, I'd hold up there and do as much digitally and over the phone as you can." She pointed to the window. "It doesn't look like the weather will let up before Christmas, and maybe that's a good thing. Be careful, Logan. I look forward to seeing how you come out of this."

Logan nodded his thanks, hurried out of her office, past Vernon's, who glared at him as he passed, fetched his things and made a quick exit.

When he reached the pavement, he felt rejuvenated, like a knight given the blessing of the Queen. He hoped to make it back to the penthouse before Daniel. Surely his new friend would know he'd gone, but at least he'd be able to tell Daniel that Fiona was on their side.

He pulled the hood of his coat over his head and ducked into the dumping snow. His mind was rolling over Fiona's words when he heard a car thump against the curb. He turned to make sure he wasn't in the way and ended up looking straight into the car.

"Get in," the driver said.

It took Logan a long moment to realize who was speaking.

"Fitzgerald," he said.

"I said, get in."

Fitzgerald moved his hand off his lap, just high enough for Logan to see the gun in the man's hand. He aimed it at Logan. The young journalist took a step back.

"Uh uh. One more step and I shoot. I swear. You do not know how much trouble you've caused."

"I didn't—"

"Get in the car. Now."

Logan looked left and right. The only pedestrian he could see was a doorman who was shoveling snow off the sidewalk. He was wearing thick ear muffs.

"Don't even think about it, kid."

Logan *did* think about. Then he looked at the gun, weighed his options, and got in the car. What else could he do?

CHAPTER 33

DANIEL BRIGGS

Jimmy Mason rented a basement apartment that smelled of mold and cat litter. So much for high class living. The thermostat was locked at a balmy 80-degrees.

Daniel let himself in when there was no answer to his knocking. As soon as he stepped inside, he knew the place was deserted. Though there were stacks and stacks of newspapers. Some piles came up to his waist. There was no Jimmy Mason around to read them.

Daniel did a cursory inspection for listening devices or video equipment. While he couldn't be one-hundred percent sure, he felt confident that the place wasn't bugged.

Second-hand mismatched silverware and broken cooking tools stuffed the kitchen drawers. One drawer contained what looked like used paper towels. It didn't look like Jimmy Mason threw anything away.

Daniel moved from the kitchen to the small living room, where the newspapers waited. The system was simple. Each pile was a different paper. *The Continental Tribune. The Wash-*

ington Exhibitor. *The London Paper*. All the top news outlets stood sentinel.

He picked up the latest edition of *The Continental Tribune* and scanned the headlines. The date printed was from five months ago. Daniel glanced at the other stacks and the dates on the top of the piles were from the same time period.

Going back to the paper in his hands, Daniel read the name of each reporter, then skimmed the story. It wasn't until the ninth page that he saw the highlighted passage:

> *Multiple sources confirm dissent within administration over crime bill.*

It was the only highlighted passage in this paper.

Daniel grabbed the next one from the stack. This time, the highlighted passage was on the sixth page.

> *A source within the administration confirmed the before mentioned conversation between the New York Attorney General and the U.S. Department of Corrections.*

Next came the top edition of *The London Paper*. The eleventh page held the highlight passage:

> *America's Department of Corrections in shambles, says source inside American government.*

Every single paper Daniel picked up had a similar passage, all having to do with crime, criminal law, U.S. prisons and the like.

Jimmy Mason was their source, Daniel realized. Mason was keeping souvenirs, trophies of his accomplishments.

He put all the papers back and walked around again, imagining the Department of Correction consultant living in the musty apartment that probably flooded if there was too much rain.

No mail in the mail slot. The thermostat is high. The heat is still running. Someone is paying the bills. But no one lives here, hasn't for some time, Daniel thought.

He closed his eyes and tried to put it all together. He called The Beast, but it didn't move, telling Daniel that there was nothing here. Standing in the middle of the apartment with his eyes shut, the Marine sniper got lucky. If it'd been a normal day in New York, with cars honking and roaring by, he probably wouldn't have heard it. Luckily it was snow-covered quiet, and when he let his senses reach out, that's when he heard it. A barely discernible beeping. Slow, like a water heater alarm in a crawl space.

Daniel moved towards the sound, noting that the beeping was not only getting louder, but faster. Just barely. By the time he got to the bedroom, not only was the heat becoming oppressive, the beeps were coming every second.

He hadn't seen it walking through before. A cigar box tucked in the corner. That's where the sound was coming from.

Carefully, but smoothly, Daniel lifted the lid. Even as he did, The Beast inside him howled a warning, and Daniel almost fell onto his backside. Lying amongst dried and rotted cigars was a device with a digital gauge that looked like a thermometer. And the red where the thermometer liquid would've been wasn't full, but almost empty. As Daniel ran for the exit, the display turned from red to green. The remote detonator triggered a chain reaction that led to the compact explosive tucked under the device, and the explosion that erupted and swallowed the entire apartment.

CHAPTER 34

DANIEL BRIGGS

"Hey, man. Are you okay?" The person's voice sounded like it was coming from inside a plastic cup a foot underwater.

"I'm fine," Daniel said, rubbing a hand on the side of his head. He looked back at the apartment. No flames, but the place lay in ruins. Strangely, it didn't look like any of the units to the side or above suffered damage.

"You're bleeding," the now-clearing voice said. Daniel nodded at the marshmallow man covered in layers of baby blue winter clothing. He was holding three tiny dogs on leashes in his arms. They stared at Daniel like good little dolls. "You should get that looked at. I'll bet you need stitches. My sister says you should never let a wound fester. Bad things happen. Gangrene. Amputation. Death."

Daniel almost laughed. The cut on his upper arm was the least of his problems.

"Do you have a phone?" Daniel asked.

"I do. Always carry it with me. Sorry, puppies, but daddy's gonna have to put you on the ground to help the poor man." He bent down and set the dogs on the ground. They tiptoed around on tamped snow like they'd been set in maple syrup. The marshmallow man held out the phone for Daniel. "Here you go."

Daniel put a hand to his head. "Sorry, do you think you can call the police?"

"Of course. Oh, I hate to say it, but this is exciting. What do you want me to tell them? Is there anyone inside? Pleeeeease tell me there wasn't anyone in there." The man shivered as he threw a pained glance at the wreckage.

"No one inside," Daniel said, staggering to his feet.

"How do you know? Were you inside? Oh my gosh, if you were—"

Think, Daniel.

"No, I was asking for donations. I live around the corner and my neighbor just died. No family. She didn't have a penny, so we're trying to collect money for her funeral."

"Oh, that's so sweet. I wish I had my wallet with me. Maybe if you—"

"I think you're right. I should go to the hospital." Daniel made a show of looking woozy, though he felt fine, just a little off kilter.

"Maybe you should wait for the ambulance. I wouldn't want you to pass out on the way there. I'd never forgive myself for letting you go. Here. lean on me if you need to."

"I'll be fine. I promise," Daniel said. "Call the police."

"Okay. But wait. You didn't tell me your name!"

Daniel was already walking away. He needed to get back to Logan. If the bad guys were getting bold enough to set off a controlled detonation in the city, who knew what they would do next?

The man in the apartment across the street watched as the baby blue marshmallow talked animatedly on his phone. The man who'd exited Mason's apartment a second before getting blown to eternity had already disappeared. That didn't matter to the man conducting surveillance. He'd already relayed the information to the team. His boss wouldn't be happy. Then again, his boss was never happy. Such was the nature of their business. When you missed your target, bad things happened. The man slung his small backpack over one shoulder and took the back stairs. It was time to hole up and get some shut eye. He had no doubt that a sleepless night was coming.

CHAPTER 35

IAN FITZGERALD

The Whitaker kid didn't engage Fitzgerald as he drove with one hand on the wheel and one hand pointing the gun at his captive. Desperate times…

Road conditions were crap. If he'd had the choice, Ian would've rather been at home, staring at a crackling fire, drinking bourbon, imagining his future. Instead, he'd just kidnapped a kid who couldn't help snooping into Fitzgerald's business.

What should've taken ten minutes, took closer to forty because of the snow. Plows were out, but the weather was faster. Fitzgerald scraped his wheels against curbs multiple times as he tried to maneuver around turns.

He pulled into the empty parking garage, grateful when his tires grabbed clean pavement. He drove up to the second floor, past the construction equipment and piles of gravel, picking a spot close to the elevator.

When he shut down the car, he swiveled in his seat.

"No sudden moves. Got me?"

"Yeah," Logan Whitaker said, staring at the gun.

"You're in a lot of trouble, kid. A lot."

By the look on Whitaker's face, the kid understood that fact and then some.

"Get out of the car. Slowly."

Fitzgerald pretended like he knew how to hold a man at gunpoint. He was no criminal. At least Pilson had put him through a weekend of basic gun training. Before that, the closest Fitzgerald had ever been to a gun was sitting on a Fourth of July float next to a cop in his hometown as a kid.

Whitaker followed the order, giving Fitzgerald enough time to move around the car, press the gun into the kid's back, and push him towards the elevators.

"If we run into anyone, act normal," Fitzgerald said, realizing how silly the words sounded. "Press the up button."

Whitaker reached out and pressed the elevator's up button. When the door opened, a man and a woman were standing inside. Fitzgerald tensed until the woman said, "We're going up to the seventh floor, Mr. Fitzgerald."

He nodded and pushed Whitaker into the elevator. The woman saw the gun in his hand and frowned.

"You left me no choice," he said, ignoring her stare. Fitzgerald was paying for them. At least they'd agreed to secure a place to interrogate Whitaker, and they even promised to stand guard, though the woman was very clear that she and her team would not lay a hand on his captive.

The seventh floor was all concrete and drywall. Bits of gravel crunched under their steps as they walked down the hall. The male contractor opened a door and led them inside. There was a small cooler and two chairs sitting under the exposed ceiling and jury-rigged lighting.

"There's water in the cooler," the woman said. "We'll be outside."

The security detail left and Fitzgerald thought about ringing the other team he'd mobilized to monitor Jimmy Mason's apartment. He'd told them to use any means necessary to keep snoopers off his back. Pilson's files said they were on time and lethal. Fitzgerald trusted Pilson's judgement, and since he hadn't yet heard from the second team, assumed the trap was still set.

"Sit down," he told Whitaker.

Whitaker sat down.

I should've brought rope, Fitzgerald thought. The gun would do.

He pulled the second chair away from Whitaker, took a seat, and rested the gun on his leg, still pointing at the journalist.

"You couldn't leave it alone, could you?"

Whitaker straightened up.

"I've got friends. They know how to find me."

Fitzgerald laughed. "Oh, you mean the friends who were going to talk to Jimmy Mason? Let me give you a preview." He made an exploding gesture with his free hand. "You won't have friends for long. I'll let you stay alive until I get the call. You know, so you can share in the good news."

Whitaker's posture wilted.

"You thought you were so smart, kid. But you had no idea what you were stepping into. Any regrets?" Fitzgerald was enjoying his new role. Intoxicating power coursed through him.

"I don't want to talk to you."

"Oh, you're going to talk to me. You're going to tell me exactly what you know and who you've told. If not, your mother will receive a unique Christmas gift: your head on a Spode platter."

"You leave her out of this."

"Why? You brought her into it the minute you stuck your nose where it didn't belong. Why couldn't you take the hint?"

"Because what you're doing is wrong!"

Fitzgerald smiled. "And what is it you think I'm doing?

Come on, impress me with your investigative skills. Show me why Fiona thinks you're so special."

Something ran across Whitaker's face. He was about to speak when a loud crash sounded from the hallway. His eyes flashed to the door. The first sound was followed by muffled grunts and what could have been a snapping of wood. At least that's what Fitzgerald thought.

Fitzgerald pulled out his phone and texted the woman,

What's going on out there?

She replied a moment later.

The muffin man...

The muffin man?

he texted back. It had to be a typo or autocorrect.

Yeah, the one who lives on Drury Lane.

What the—

The door opened, and a man who Fitzgerald did not recognize sauntered into the room. There was something about his face though. Had he met the man before? He held a knife in his right hand, and at first he thought the security team had reconsidered helping him with the interrogation. Then he saw the blood splattered on the man's neck.

"Who are—"

Before Fitzgerald could react, the stranger flicked the blade, and it embedded in Fitzgerald's right shoulder. The gun dropped from his hand and Fitzgerald let out a howl of pain. The man rushed over and clamped a hand over his mouth.

"Shhh. You don't want the muffin man to hear you," the man hissed.

Fitzgerald had never felt such pain. He thought he might pass out. It was nothing compared to the torture when the man reached over and dug the knife deeper into his shoulder.

"Don't go passing out on me, Fitzy. We've got loads to discuss."

Fitzgerald's eyes flicked to Whitaker, who was watching with a hint of amusement. Whitaker said, "Don't look at me. He's the one running the show now."

Fitzgerald's mouth moved under the man's hand. He was trying to ask for air. But instead, his eyes rolled back in his head and he slumped in the chair. Matthew Wilcox eased him to the ground and said, "Well, that was easier than I thought. Now grab his legs. We need to get the hell outta here."

CHAPTER 36

LOGAN WHITAKER

Logan tried to shake the image of the two dead guards from his head. The woman's body was especially gruesome, with her head twisted around like a broken marionette.

"Did you have to kill them?" Logan whispered as Matthew sped towards the parking garage exit.

"How 'bout a little appreciation, Logan? A thank you would be nice. It's a good thing Mr. Fitzgerald didn't blow your kneecaps off. I'm pretty sure he was about to." He motioned to the bound and unconscious man lying in the backseat. "I can't wait to blow *his* kneecaps off."

"I think we should talk to Daniel."

The assassin laughed. "Daniel? Who saved your ass? Mr. High and Mighty or me? You might think I'm nuts-o, but I'm the one who tracked Fitzy down and figured out what he was about to do to you."

Logan didn't want to seem afraid, though he was, so he laid in with questions.

"How did you find me?"

"I have my ways."

"Tell me about them," Logan said.

"You wouldn't understand, newsy. I saw the look on your face when you almost tripped over the bodies. You were gonna faint. Admit it."

"I was not."

"Okay, then you peed in your pants a little. Didn't you?"

Matthew swerved the car and almost went out of the garage on two wheels. Logan held on to the door. When he looked in the backseat, Matthew noticed Fitzgerald pushed against the opposite side of the car in a heap.

"Maybe you should slow down," Logan said.

"And maybe you should thank your lucky stars. This ain't a fairy tale, Logan."

"What about the bodies? You can't just leave them there."

Matthew tapped the side of his head. "There you go figuring stuff out again. I'm proud of you, little buddy. Maybe you weren't gonna pass out, vomit or pee your pants. As much as I'd like to continue your education of all things Me, we need to get you back to the penthouse."

"What about Fitzgerald?" Logan asked.

"You let me take care of him, okay? I'm sure Daniel will love to know why you snuck out of the safe zone after he went looking for Jimmy Mason."

"How did you know that?"

"I told you, Mr. Reporter, I have my ways. Now, hold on, I've always wanted to drive some else's car through the snow. Bet I don't hit one fire hydrant!"

Matthew dropped Logan off at the front door. He hadn't hit a single fire hydrant. He had scared two kids having a snowball fight, one old lady yelling for her cat, and a cop whose cruiser got stuck in the snow.

"Tell Daniel to make me a leftover plate for dinner. I might be late."

The assassin sped off, the backend of Fitzgerald's car fishtailing on the slick street.

Logan looked up at the building and realized he didn't want to admit his mistake to Daniel. Daniel wasn't the sort of man Logan wanted to let down.

Daniel was applying a large bandage to his upper arm when Logan walked into the kitchen. Bloody gauze and a bottle of rubbing alcohol were on the counter.

"What happened?" Logan asked. "Did you go to Jimmy Mason's?"

"I did." Daniel pressed the bandage so it would seal, and then lowered his sleeve. "I was worried about you."

The funny thing was, nothing in Daniel's tone or facial expression gave the "what the hell have you been up to and I'm disappointed" vibe. But Logan felt bad.

"I had to do something. I'm sorry I didn't tell." Then he told Daniel everything, from his conversation at work with Fiona, to his kidnapping at the hands of Ian Fitzgerald, and finally, his savior, Matthew the assassin. "I should've listened to you. I'm sorry."

"It's done," Daniel said. "And though I would not have chosen that exact path, I think it helped us."

"It did?"

"I told you I had a hunch. And that hunch was that Matthew knew more than he let on. Like knowing exactly where to be to help you. It's too convenient. He works with a level of calm that impresses even me. But it's like he's been one step ahead of us."

Logan took a seat. "Are you saying he's working with Fitzgerald?"

"I don't think it's that bad. But if I've learned anything about Matthew, it's that he has his own motives, and those motives don't always align with the good guys. At least not completely. I wouldn't be surprised if Matthew actually did some of the things we thought Fitzgerald did."

"But why?"

"In Matthew lingo: why not? You and I think on fairly linear terms. We know how to be creative, but we like it when two and two add up to four. Matthew doesn't think that way. You throw a monkey wrench in his plans and he reaches into the tool chest, grabs three more wrenches, a hammer and a handful of screws and throws them in after you. Rhyme and reason don't exist in his thinking."

Logan thought about Daniel's revelation. Then said, "So why haven't you killed him?"

Something flickered in Daniel's eyes. "As I've told you before, Matthew has his uses."

Then it clicked.

"Wait a minute, you like the chaos too." That's what he'd seen in Daniel's look.

"Sometimes. I'm working on that," Daniel said.

Logan would have to remember that fact. Two killers with a penchant for destruction.

"So, how do we use him now? He's got Fitzgerald. I wouldn't be surprised if he dumped the guy's body in the Hudson by now."

Daniel shook his head. "No. That would be too easy. And Matthew doesn't do easy. He needs something from Fitzgerald. And we need to figure out what that is."

"What if it's just fun to him, that he wants to see Fitzgerald bleed out and nothing else?"

Daniel shrugged. "Then we deal with it as it comes."

CHAPTER 37

IAN FITZGERALD

Someone was stroking his head. The memory of his mother came to him, a day when he'd stayed home from school with the flu and she'd nursed him back to health with homemade chicken broth and saltine crackers.

"There, there," said a voice.

Ian almost asked, "Mom?" But his mind deduced that it wasn't a female voice. It was a man.

He tensed. The movement triggered a chain reaction that sent a spike of agony into his shoulder. He moaned, and the head stroking came back.

"Now, now. It's going to be okay."

Ian tried to open his eyes and see. Why couldn't he see?!

"Am I blind?" he croaked through the pain. Saliva ran down his cheeks when he turned his head from side to side.

"Do you want to be blind?" the male voice asked.

"No! Oh, Lord, please let me—"

"I didn't expect that from you," the voice said. "You don't strike me as a religious fellow, what with all the manipulation and blackmail. Then again, historians say that some of the greatest gangsters of the early twentieth century never missed a day at church. I wonder how that lines up with God's plan."

That voice. It took Ian's brain time to focus through the pain and mind swirl.

"You," he said.

"Me?" the voice said.

He's going to kill me. Oh, please...

"What do you want? Is it money? I have money!"

"I don't want your money. I want you to live a short and exciting life. I patched up your shoulder. Probably hurts like hell, but you'll live. At least for now."

Ian wanted to see the man. He tried to move his good arm, but he realized it was pinned to his side. Something about the not seeing made this even more terrifying.

Think, Ian. Think!

"I have friends. Lots of friends. You need something, anything, they can get it for you," Ian blubbered. "Do you have something for the pain? My shoulder is killing me."

Ian felt hands on the side of his head and he imagined his skull being crushed. His skull wasn't crushed. But the blindfold came off and Ian squinted to look into the amused eyes of his captor, the man who'd embedded a knife in his shoulder.

"There. Is that better?" the man asked.

Ian nodded, wincing. Any movement elicited jolting pain everywhere around his shoulder, like that whole side of his body was being electrocuted.

"What do you want?" Ian asked, trying to gather his wits and nerves.

"I told you. I want you to live a short and exciting life. I'm going to help you, Ian Fitzgerald. I really am. You have to trust me. Trust means everything to me."

The man grabbed him by the front of the shirt and yanked him with surprising strength into a seated position. Ian swooned with pain and almost passed out.

"Hey, focus on me," the man said.

"I need to lie down."

"You'll be fine."

Ian looked around the darkened room. That's when it hit him. He was in his own room. In his own bed. The realization almost knocked him unconscious.

"Here's what's gonna happen, Fitzy. You don't mind if I call you Fitzy, do you?"

Ian shook his head, thinking that Gregory Worthington might find this man amusing. "I'm gonna leave," the man said.

He waited for his captor to say more. When he didn't, staring into Ian's eyes instead, Ian couldn't help but ask, "And then what?"

"I have wired your house to explode in exactly five minutes." You'll be tied to the bed and won't be able to get out. You'll enjoy your last minutes on Earth like a steak sizzling on a grill."

Ian's eyes went wide and tears clouded his vision.

"I'm kidding!" The man wiped Ian's eyes with the duvet. "You should see the look on your face, Fitzy. I could've sworn you had a heart attack. Now what would that do to my promise of keeping you alive? Nothing good! To the plan. I'm leaving and I want you to go back to work."

"You're not going to interrogate me?"

"Do you want me to?" Ian shook his head. "Good. Cuz I'm not in the mood to twist your nipples and clamp your nads to a car battery. That's so Miami Vice. Have any questions?"

There were too many questions.

Why are you doing this?

Who are you?

Why are you letting me live?

Ian figured it was best to keep the questions to himself. If this lunatic wanted to let him go, so be it. He'd hop on a plane and disappear before the sun rose the next day.

"One more thing," the man said. His hand rested on Ian's wounded shoulder. His thumbed pressed, and Ian shuddered involuntarily. "Don't run. I'll know. And you won't like what happens when I catch you."

Ian believed the man. Just to be sure he asked, "You want me to get back to work?"

"That's right."

"And you know what I do?"

"Of course."

Ian didn't ask, "What's in it for you?" He assumed he'd find out soon enough. Maybe he could find a way out. Escape was impossible if he were dead. So for now, he'd try to stay alive. *Play along, Ian.*

"How do we stay in touch?"

"I'll be watching." The man slid off the bed and straightened his shirt. "I'll let you know when I need you."

"What do I call you?"

"You don't."

The man walked out of Ian's bedroom, and for the next thirty minutes, Ian waited for his house to explode. It did not explode. But his mind whirred with images of death, pain, and the strange man who Ian knew would happily string him up like a pig and roast him over a low burning fire.

CHAPTER 38

GREGORY WORTHINGTON

Six television screens each showed a different news feed. They were all on mute and he wasn't watching anymore.

"Mr. Worthington, the front gate says Mr. Fitzgerald is back," the butler announced from the office door.

"Tell him to go away." His voice slurred with vodka.

"Sir, he says he has evidence."

Worthington rose from his chair, almost knocking over the bottles on the table. "You tell him if he ever comes to my home again, I will—"

"Sir." The butler had been with the Worthington family since Gregory was in his teens. He was more like a stern uncle than a servant.

"Fine. Tell me."

"Might you not have a word with Mr. Fitzgerald, put his mind at ease, maybe send him on a hunt that will keep him busy until you've had time to better craft a plan to deal with him permanently?"

It took a moment for the suggestion to filter through the day of drinking.

"Fine. Why not? But bring me my gun. No! My father's gun. The one in the bedroom safe."

"Yes, sir."

The butler disappeared and Worthington poured himself more vodka. He didn't even worry about the soda or the lime anymore.

When Fitzgerald tramped into the room, he looked more than a little frazzled.

"You don't give up, do you?" Worthington asked bitterly.

"I don't have a choice! Why did you shut me out?"

Worthington frowned, walked over to a more comfortable chair, and sat down.

"I was dissuaded," he said.

"Dissuaded? Dissuaded from what?"

"From cavorting with you!" Worthington screamed, pointing with the hand with the drink, sloshing half of it on the floor. "Look at what you made me do."

"I need a drink," Fitzgerald said. That's when Worthington noticed his friend's arm in a cheap sling.

"What happened to your arm?"

"Don't ask. I had to beg my doctor to send a prescription to the drugstore."

Fitzgerald grabbed a glass and filled it full with vodka. "Probably shouldn't be mixing this with pain meds, but who the hell cares?"

He took his drink to the seat next to Worthington, sat down with pained effort, and stared at the television screens. For a time, they drank and said nothing. Worthington had been so scared after his run-in at Fitzy's office that he'd blamed it all on his friend. But now, sitting safely behind a vodka brain, layers of machine gun security, and the bedrock of his family home, his mind shifted. He looked at his friend, who'd obviously been through some ordeal. Worthington was curious to understand what that was.

"Are you going to tell me why you're here?" Worthington asked.

"Would you believe I have nowhere else to go?"

"Isn't that a line from *Officer and a Gentleman*?"

"Who cares?" Fitzy gulped more vodka and kept his morose gaze on the televisions.

"Is it the business?"

"You could say that."

"What happened to your arm?"

"A lunatic stabbed me with a knife."

Worthington laughed so hard that his drink came out of his nose.

"I'm glad I could be so entertaining," Fitzy said.

"I'm sorry. You look awful. Truly. The worst I've ever seen you."

"Even worse than the time I stole my dad's mint schnapps and drank the whole bottle before school?"

"Yes, Fitzy, worse than that."

They shared a smile.

"Why did you cut me off?" Fitzy asked. His eyes were pleading, like Gregory's cold shoulder had caused the entire world to turn on the man.

"Someone threatened me."

"Who threatened you?"

"A man at your office."

"What? When? Who was it?"

"Yesterday. He was the security guard at the entrance. Although, I believe that he masqueraded as your doorman."

"We have one chief guard and his name is Arturo. Heavy set. Eyes close together?"

"No. That wasn't him."

Fitzy's eyes narrowed.

"Hold on. Did the guy have a weird sense of humor, maybe throw nonsense one-liners at you?"

Worthington sat up straighter. "Yes. Who is he?"

Fitzy pointed to his wounded shoulder. "I think it's the same guy who did this."

Worthington's brain went from fuzz to clear. "Why did he stab you?"

"I don't know. He could've killed me. He killed two of my security contractors. I'm sure of it."

"Who did you piss off, Fitzy?"

His friend shook his head. "I don't know."

"But he let you go?"

"He did. He said I should get back to work."

"That doesn't make any sense," Worthington said. "I know you've kept me in the dark about what you do behind the scenes, but I think it's time you tell me everything."

"You think that's smart? I don't want to get you into—"

"I'm already in it! He threatened me too!"

Fitzy nodded. "Fine. You're right. And I'm sorry. I didn't mean for this to happen. I don't even know why it happened."

"Let me help you. And if I can't help you, I have friends who can."

Fitzy sipped his drink, thinking. "Okay. Here's where I think it started…"

He told Worthington everything. About arranging for Niles Petersen to be killed. About Logan Whitaker being at the scene by some stupid coincidence. About Pilson making the mistake of not dealing with Whitaker when he had the chance. He, a good journalist, stated the facts, added a little guessing as to why it might've happened, but didn't commit to a solid hypothesis. Then he told the most nefarious aspects of how he'd expanded the operation. When he finished telling the tale, he stood up and refilled his drink. Though he didn't say it, Worthington was impressed. Fitzy had never been one to take risks in the past. Maybe a little tomfoolery, but nothing like this. Though Fitzy didn't say it, Worthington's mind instantly comprehended why Fitzy had done it. And he'd been oblivious to it all along. Fitzy wanted power. That was fine with Worthington, to a point. His family had not risen to its current prominence by handing out kingdoms to those lower on the social rung. No. Lordships might be gifts, but never the kingdom. They could rescind a lordship.

"Do you think we can find this funny fellow?" Worthington asked.

"Mr. Crazy Stab and Let Me Go?"

"Yes."

Fitzy laughed. "I think he's crazy enough to do it again. He said he's watching. I believe him."

Worthington pressed a button on the table and the butler appeared.

"Sir?"

"Bring two pitchers of water. And coffee. It's going to be a long night. Have them make a light dinner," Worthington ordered.

"Yes, Mr. Worthington."

Head clear. Vodka put down. Worthington's mind tackled the dilemma with relish. By the time the food arrived, he'd outlined an audacious plan that, he believed, had an eighty-five percent chance of success. Not only did he want to stay alive, now that he'd had time to think about it, he wanted to take a more active role in Fitzy's business. He'd learn the ropes and help with connections. Then, if Fitzy wore out his usefulness, Fitzgerald & Muse would be integrated into the Worthington empire. But that was a decision for another day. Today, they needed to find and kill the man responsible for bringing terror to their door.

CHAPTER 39

MATTHEW WILCOX

Daniel and Logan each gave him the same look when he returned to the penthouse.

"What? Do I have snow on my face?" Wilcox asked, swiping his hands over his nose and cheeks.

"Where is Fitzgerald?" Daniel asked.

Wilcox stripped off his coat and hat and threw them on the floor.

"I let him go."

"You let him go?" Logan asked, incredulous.

"Is there an echo in here? Yes, I let him go."

"Why? I thought you were—"

"You thought I was going to what? Kill him?" Wilcox laughed. "You can't solve everything with death, kid. I hope Daniel didn't plant that idea in your head. Anyone need a beer? Fresca for you, Dan Dan?"

He headed for the kitchen but Daniel cut him off, rising from his chair and saying, "We know about Pilson."

"Who's Pilson? You sure you don't want a Fresca? Seems

like you could use one. I'll stick to a wee bit of alcohol. Logan, you in?"

Daniel radiated contempt as he walked at the assassin.

"You know who Pilson is. You killed him and his partner. Why?"

"Gee, I don't know. Maybe because I enjoy saving your ass?"

"Not good enough. Why did you do it and why didn't you tell us?"

Daniel was as unglued as Wilcox had ever seen him. The assassin's inner smile glowed.

"Maybe I forgot? Maybe I just didn't feel like telling you. Who cares?"

He and Daniel were face to face now.

"What's your game, Matthew?"

"I don't know. What's your game, Dani—"

Daniel's hand shot out and grabbed the assassin by the throat. Wilcox didn't move to stop him. He just stood there and glared right back. *Go ahead,* his eyes said. *Do it.*

He counted down half a minute before Daniel let go.

"Woof. You been working on your grip strength? If not, then you should. My granny could've done better."

Daniel didn't move. Wilcox pondered ending it all right then and there. But what fun would that be? He was just getting warmed up.

"Okay. Fine. I killed Pilson and his pal. Then I killed another guy who came with the fat man named Moretti. I killed the chick and her number two when I rescued Logan. I chucked a knife from halfway across the room and stuck it in Fitzgerald's shoulder. There. Are you happy? I feel like I just went to confession. Are you going to absolve me of my sins, Snake Eyes? How many Hail Marys do I need to pray? Do you have rosary beads handy?"

Daniel walked back to his seat.

"Wait a second," Wilcox said. "I tell you all that and you don't give me anything back? What the hell is wrong with you? At least Cal fights back."

Daniel looked at him for a long time. Then he said, "Do you want me to fight back, Matthew? Is that what you've wanted all along? Because I can make a phone call right now and my friends will be more than happy to take you to a place where you'll never get to see the sky or sun ever again. We had a deal, remember?"

"What deal?" Logan asked.

"It's not like I signed a contract or anything," Wilcox said.

"No. You agreed to be on our side. Always. If not, we reserve the right to dissolve our working relationship and let the U.S. Government have you. Is that what you want?"

Wilcox wanted many things. One of those things was not being locked up in a super secret U.S. prison. He'd heard the food was atrocious.

"Okay. You got me. What do you want me to say? Sorry?"

"I know you're not sorry, so don't waste the breath. From now on, you're with me or you're gone. Got it?"

Wilcox rolled his eyes. "Yes, sir, Mr. Marine, sir. I really need to get you to an improv class. I swear, it would help your delivery immensely."

Daniel ignored him. "We've got one day to get this wrapped up."

"One day? Why one day?" Wilcox asked.

"Because the day after tomorrow is Christmas, and I'd like to make sure Logan gets home in time to spend the day with his mother. You have a problem with that?"

"No. But I have one request."

"What is it?"

"You let me go in first. You can be right behind me, but I wanna go in first."

For the first time that night, Daniel smiled at the assassin.

"Fine by me. I don't mind jumping over your corpse to take out the bad guys."

They shared a laugh at that. Logan just sat there, too amazed by the interaction to have any reaction at all.

CHAPTER 40

LOGAN WHITAKER

"Are you ready?" Daniel asked.

It was morning. They huddled under an awning in view of the Fitzgerald & Muse office building. Snow continued to blanket the city and only the bravest of the New Yorkers plodded their way through snowdrifts, waist deep in many places.

"I'm ready," Logan said, suppressing a shiver as he looked at their target.

"Remember, I'll be close by. So will Matthew."

"How do you know he'll want to see me?" Logan asked.

"Just tell him what we talked about. And try your best. I trust you."

Matthew yawned. "I'm not sure I do. Seriously, how about I run in there, nab the goober, toss him out the window into your waiting arms, and we can electroshock what we need out of him?"

"Because that's not the plan," Daniel said.

"Plan, schplan. You're no fun."

Daniel ignored him and focused on Logan. "You've got this."

Logan nodded. He wasn't sure if he had anything. But he'd try.

By the time he reached the front door, fluffy snow caked the front of his body. He dusted himself off before walking through the door.

"May I help you?" the security guard said, eying him warily.

"Yikes. Sure is cold out there!" Logan said, trying to shake his nerves loose.

"Yes, sir. May I help you?" The man's hand slid to his hip.

"I'm here to see Mr. Muse."

"Do you have an appointment?"

"I do not."

"Then might I suggest you come back when you have one?"

"I would, but it's Christmas. And I can't deliver the news over the phone. It has to be in person. There's always somebody listening."

The guard gave him a hard look, picked up the house phone, punched a button, and waited. Logan watched the man's eyes, which never left him. "Mr. Muse, I have a gentleman here to see you." A pause to listen. Then to Logan, "What is your name, sir?"

This was the tricky part. "Jimmy Mason."

The guard relayed the name and nodded his head. "Yes, sir. I'll send him up."

He hung up the phone, slowly. "Seems like an odd time to pay a visit."

"Work hath no time like the present," Logan said, hoping the man who Wilcox admitted to hogtying and stripping to his underwear on a previous visit would, in fact, let him pass.

The guard grunted and pointed towards the elevator.

Once Logan was in the elevator, he took a deep breath and texted Daniel.

I'm in.

Good work. We're just outside.

Even though two formidable men were waiting to run to his rescue, Logan couldn't help but feel alone. If this was what journalism looked like, he wasn't sure he wanted it.

The ding of the elevator startled him. When the doors opened, Marty Muse was waiting.

"You're not Jimmy," Muse said. He gripped the phone in his hand and started to raise it.

"Wait! Mr. Muse, please."

The plan was to feed Muse the story they'd concocted, all to flush Fitzgerald from hiding and expose the entire scheme. But when Logan looked into the man's honest eyes, something inside him turned. He had to tell the truth.

"You're from *The Continental Ledger*," Muse said.

"Yes, sir. But I'm not here for a story. I promise. I'm here to help."

"Help? Help with what?"

Logan took a deep breath and tried to picture Fiona standing next to him, pushing him to do the right thing.

"Mr. Muse, how much do you know about Ian Fitzgerald."

"What sort of question is that? Young man, should I call Fiona Graves? Because I think your very presence is—"

"Sir, I believe that Ian Fitzgerald is not only manipulating your sources for his own purposes, but he's had several of them killed and replaced."

Muse's eyebrows rose.

"That's impossible."

Logan had to convince the man. He tried to compare what

he knew about Fitzgerald with the man who was standing in front of him. Logan assumed Muse was a good man with terrible taste in clothing. He wondered if the suit was second hand. The dots in Logan's mind connected.

"Have there been any recent windfalls for your firm, Mr. Muse?"

Muse didn't answer immediately, but Logan thought he saw a hint of recognition in the man's eyes.

"I can't see how that's any of your concern."

Logan pressed harder.

"Sir, has Ian Fitzgerald told you that the firm is on better financial footing, that he's courting new clients and investigating expansion?"

That one hit home. It was like Logan dumped a bucket of ice water on the man's head.

"What... I don't understand. How do you know... what is—"

"Mr. Muse, I promise I'm not here to cause you trouble."

"But what you said. If it's true, if Ian... it can't be true."

Muse was running down the most obvious path, toward the pit of oblivion for his firm and his career. Logan needed to throw him a lifeline, quick.

"Sir, what if there's a way to fix it?" Think fast, Logan, this guy's gonna crumble.

"Fix it? How on Earth could we fix murder?"

That's when the answer came to Logan.

"It was all his fault. It doesn't have to be yours," he said.

Muse's whole body was shaking.

"It's *our* firm. I can't bury the story. I'm a journalist to my core. I have a responsibility—"

"And so do I! But a person much smarter than myself once told me that sometimes a measured approach is how you deliver the truth."

Muse stared at him. "Fiona told you that, didn't she?"

"Yes, sir, she did."

"Does she know about this?"

"No, sir."

Muse shook his head. "What are we going to do? Everything I've built. How can I face my wife, my colleagues?"

Logan remembered his father saying that you should never make promises if you couldn't uphold them. But Logan knew that in this case, there was no other way.

"Mr. Muse, I promise that my friends and I will make everything right again."

Muse's eyes lit up for the first time. He asked with genuine curiosity, "Who are your friends?"

CHAPTER 41

DANIEL BRIGGS

"You did what?!" Wilcox flared, lunging for the front of Logan's coat.

Daniel stepped between them.

"Lay hands on him again…"

Wilcox raised his hands in the air.

"You're both crazy, you know that?! You think I'm nuts. You're both nuts with a capital N *and* Z."

Despite Daniel's displeasure with Logan going off script, he couldn't do anything to change it now.

"Why did you tell him the truth?" Daniel asked.

"I don't know. I just... I guess I felt like it would work better than a lie."

Wilcox laughed and said, "You stupid kid. Lies always work! Always!"

"Let him speak," Daniel said.

Logan eyed Wilcox and went on. "I don't want Mr. Muse to get hurt. This wasn't his fault. And I know what you're going to say, Matthew, that he's complicit and he should've known what his partner was doing. But not everyone thinks like you. Some of us trust others."

Daniel waited for Wilcox to respond. He could see the assassin chewing the words in his head. To Daniel's surprise, Wilcox clapped his hands together and said, "Well, kid, I gotta hand it to you. I don't know if that was the bravest or stupidest thing you could've done. But you tipped a domino and now it's just a matter of time to see what you knock over next. Snake Eyes, you with me?" Wilcox held a hand up, expecting a high five. Daniel didn't give it to him.

"While I appreciate Matthew's newfound excitement," Daniel thought that Wilcox's abrupt turnaround was anything but unselfish, "I think we should tread carefully. We can only guess what Muse will do with the information you dumped in his lap."

Logan perked up. "Shoot. I almost forgot! That's the best part. Mr. Muse said we're welcome to his files. He wants to help us in identifying the compromised sources and the ones he can still trust.

"And which ones are dead," Wilcox said.

"Sure. There's that too. But he's giving us full access. Isn't that a good thing?"

Wilcox gave him a grim smile. "Not if you want to get home to mommy in time for Christmas hot cocoa. Tell me, newsie, how many files do we need to sift through in time for turkey dinner, all while figuring out a way to let the authorities nab Fitzgerald and his pals? If you can't tell by the tone of my voice, I think it's highly unlikely we do either before one of us dies of old age."

Daniel couldn't disagree. Logan's expertise in on-your-toes investigations and exploitation was nil. But the kid was trying.

"Let's see what we can find in Muse's files."

"I'm not going," Wilcox said.

"I didn't say you were."

"Let me guess, it's time for your friendly neighborhood Superman to fly home and leave the do-gooders to their do-gooding. Lame."

"No," Daniel said. "I want you to find Fitzgerald and watch him. Do not make contact. Understood?"

"Sure, sure. I won't hurt any of the wee baby hairs on his wee baby head. Promise. Cross my heart and hope to die." He raised his left pinky finger, licked it, kissed it, and drew a cross over his heart.

"Logan, let's go," Daniel said, pulled the young journalist from cover as Wilcox waved them a happy goodbye.

When they were out of earshot, Logan asked, "You sure that's a good idea, letting him go? How do you know he won't do something stupid?"

Daniel grinned. "Actually, that's exactly what I'm hoping he will do. He can't help himself. Now come on, we've got work to do."

MARTY MUSE

Marty Muse could barely see the pair walking across the street through the driving snow. He wondered who the second man was. Whitaker, the kid from *The Continental,* seemed sincere.

But still... Marty Muse had been in the media game for a long time. He was an honest man, sometimes to a fault. But he'd learned the hard way that honest men had to cover their backside the most. He knew his vulnerability.

So he picked up his phone and dialed a number from memory. When the receiver answered, Marty said quickly, "Fiona, I don't have much time. I need to tell you something in case anything happens to me. You were right. I think Ian's up to something, and I think Logan Whitaker is in on it, too."

CHAPTER 42

MARTY MUSE

The man with the blonde ponytail introduced himself as Daniel.

"I assume it's best that I don't know your last name?" Muse asked.

"Maybe for now," the man said. Marty noted how Whitaker's companion had an almost animalistic way of moving, more like he flowed, like he was one with the world around him. Through years of source acquisition and precise journalistic research, Marty Muse had a highly tuned sense of human nature. His snap judgement was that this Daniel was a good man, a man of quiet hidden power. Marty felt himself relax when he came to that settling conclusion.

"Mr. Muse, would it be okay if you gave us a walkthrough of your files? Is there a computer you'd like us to—"

"Computer?" Marty asked. "Ah, I see what you're asking." He walked over to the closet, typed in a four-digit code, and opened the door. "I run my file system the old way, gentlemen. Paper files only." Logan and Daniel shared a look.

"I can see you're concerned, but the key to unlocking the system is up here." He tapped the side of his head.

Daniel said, "While we appreciate your help, sir, I think the bigger concern is Ian Fitzgerald."

"How do you mean?"

"He knows about your file system?"

"Of course."

"Does he have access to the files?"

"When I'm here, yes."

"Has he suggested that you digitize the files?"

Marty had to think on the question. "No. Not that I recall."

"I think what Daniel is trying to say, Mr. Muse," Logan said, "is that in this day and age, a physical paper trail is much easier to cover up, or make disappear completely than a digital one."

"I guess I'd never thought of that," Marty said, the consequences of Ian's duplicity taking deeper hold. "You must think I'm stupid."

Daniel shook his head. "You're an honest man. You made an honest mistake. Why don't you show us how to best tackle the files, and we'll ask questions as we think of them? Does that sound reasonable?"

Marty's heart was in his stomach. He felt like a fool. "Of course. Ask me anything you'd like." He hitched up his pants and stepped to the filing cabinet. "Let's start with the beginning."

It took Marty Muse half an hour to show them his system. Along the way, Logan and Daniel chimed in with insightful questions. By the time he stepped away from the filing cabinets, Marty felt like the two men had a firm grasp of the thing.

"Might I suggest you begin with the end? Now that I've had time to think on it, Ian was more vocal about specific requests. I'll tab those files if you think it's important."

"That would be helpful. Thank you," Daniel said. "Logan, is there anything else Mr. Muse can do to make this go faster?"

Logan took a moment to think. Marty wished he had the young man's enthusiasm. Though they were discussing the death of men and women he had recruited, the fear didn't seem to faze the young journalist. Marty couldn't remember ever feeling that way. Had he?

"Can you think of any similarities between Niles Petersen and Jimmy Mason?" Logan asked.

Marty's heart thudded as the faces of the two sources came to mind. If they were dead, was it his fault?

"Niles Petersen worked for the Department of Homeland Security. Jimmy Mason was a consultant of sorts for the Federal Department of Corrections. I recruited them years apart, Mason first. He was a reliable source. We don't keep track of such things, but I'm sure he had one of the highest counts of media mentions, all anonymous, of course. Petersen was young, ambitious. Sometimes ambition is good in a source. Sometimes it makes them greedy. No, I can't think of what could make them similar."

"What about monetary compensation, Mr. Muse? Did they have a similar attitude towards making money as sources?" Logan asked.

"I stay as far away from money as I can. My wife takes care of the family finances. You should've seen my credit card debt when we got married. No, money is Ian's domain." Marty realized where Logan's line of questioning meant to go as he finished his explanation. "I made another mistake, didn't I?"

"This might be a good thing," Daniel said. His tone reassured Marty. What was it about the gravitas in the man's voice? "Money leaves a trail. When we bring this to the authorities, they'll start there. If you had nothing to do with the money, it will be easier to show a judge that you had nothing to do with the Ian's illegal activities."

"A judge? Do you think it will come to that?"

Neither Logan nor Daniel answered. Instead, Logan looked at his companion and said, "I'm going to start with what worked last time. Like Mr. Muse said, I'll pull the sources that Fitzgerald requested, and I'll do a social media and general Internet search. If I don't find any personal images or basic presence, I'll flag them and we can add them to our must-look pile."

"I'm sorry," Marty said. "I must sound dense when I ask this, but what do you aim to accomplish? Why wouldn't we just hand this over to the authorities now?"

Marty didn't want to go to jail. He didn't want to stand in front of a judge. He didn't want to be scrutinized. He just wanted to do his job. Would he even have a job after this fiasco?

Daniel answered. "Once we hand this over to the authorities, word will spread. When it does, those parties responsible for hiring tainted sources will run and hide behind an army of lawyers. They may even come after you. We can't let that happen."

"But why not? Isn't that how this works?"

Marty watched as fire came to Daniel's eyes, making the breath catch in the older man's throat. Daniel said calmly, "Because in my world we don't let the bad guys get away, Mr. Muse."

CHAPTER 43

IAN FITZGERALD

Ian was tired, yet hopeful. A long night of deliberating with Gregory had given him a much better picture of the resources his old friend had at his disposal. Billions helped. But it was the friends in government agencies that made the Worthingtons so powerful.

"The government has a vested interest in protecting its citizens of means," Gregory had explained, like the FBI was on speed dial.

Ian let his friend do most of the talking. When his eyes finally went blurry and his mind could no longer follow the twists and turns Gregory kept weaving, he begged for a guest room where he could get some much needed rest. Even though he was exhausted, he'd still lain in bed, wide awake, wishing he could sleep. He ended up taking a sleeping pill that knocked him out until 10am.

He was in the kitchen, putting in his brunch order with Gregory's cook, when the man of the house appeared in a silk robe and leather flip flops.

"Did you sleep?" Gregory asked, leaning over the cook's

shoulder to inspect the omelette. "Another minute and it's ready." Gregory liked to think of himself as an accomplished chef, thanks to a summer spent in Paris where he dated women who all worked in high-end restaurants.

"I finally fell asleep at five. You?"

Gregory snorted. "I don't have time for sleep." Ian knew that meant his friend was riding serenely on one or more of his assortment of pills. Though Ian enjoyed booze, he'd never understood the need for pills. But the circle Gregory Worthington ran in seemed to have a pill for every occasion. "I made calls while you slept. Grab your breakfast and bring it to my office."

Gregory left the kitchen and Ian waited for his omelette. He'd been starving when he walked in. His friend's appearance reminded Ian why he was here, and he almost left the proffered meal, bedecked with a dollop of homemade sour cream and a metal bowl piled with fresh-cut fruit, on the counter.

"Thank you," Ian said to cook, and went to join Gregory.

His host was watching the snow fall through the huge office window when he entered. "You look awful, Fitzy."

Ian was in no mood for Gregory's nagging.

"Why don't you just tell me about your calls," Ian said.

"Suit yourself. But if you'd like a little pick me up..." When Ian didn't take the invitation, Gregory shrugged. "Fine. Let me see. It took some doing, but I was able to have several conversations. You don't need to know which agencies I contacted, but you do need to understand that the time of year and the weather make this a rather delicate thing to accomplish."

"We're talking about killing people. Not putting on a parade," Ian said, forcing himself to take a bite of his food.

"You sound like a man with vast experience. Tell me Fitzy, do you think you'd look better in an orange jumpsuit or tan?"

"They can never tie the deaths back to me."

"I thought we discussed this. Does that even matter? The gentleman who so rudely inserted himself into our lives, a ruthlessly crass individual who I believe has much more experience with killing than you ever will, is probably at this very moment planning for the way he is going to get us. *That's* what I'm concerned about, not the authorities."

Ian wanted to hire more guns to find the mystery funny man and Whitaker and kill them both. Gregory didn't believe that was necessary, that using federal authorities who could make the kill legal (he said there were easy ways to make that happen) would not only be more poetic, but would enhance their network of sources. Gregory explained that poorly paid federal employees, while unwilling to take outright payments, would enjoy the resources of a man like Gregory Worthington, especially if there was the suggestion that some future post-federal job might be waiting.

"I don't want to die either," Ian said, his appetite gaining as he dug into the perfectly cooked omelette.

"Then we're on the same page!" Gregory turned away from the window and sat on the edge of his massive desk. Ian's stomach turned when he looked up at his friend. He knew that look. The other shoe was about to drop. "If I do this for you, then you have to do something for me."

Ian somehow swallowed what now tasted like cardboard in his mouth.

"What do you want?"

"Not much. At least not in the grand scheme. Call it a little bite. A morsel. A wee nibble off the—"

"Gregory."

Gregory shook his head and his eyes bore into Ian's. "I know what you were trying to do, and you almost got away with it."

Ian wanted to squirm. His old roommate always had that effect on him. "I don't know what you're talking about."

"You sound like you're seventeen again. You know very

well that in building your network of sources, coupled with the power of new clients, my friends, you could possess a bastion of power that might not only sway public opinion, but markets, policy, and even human life. Am I close?"

"You're saying I was wrong?"

Gregory laughed. "No, Fitzy! You weren't wrong with *what* you were doing. You were wrong in *how* you were doing it. If you'd come to me sooner, we could've avoided all this unpleasantry. I give you credit for seeing the potential, but you needed a partner who could help you see the grander vision become reality. But I think I understand why you did it on your own. Maybe you wanted something all to yourself. Maybe you wanted recognition because you never got any before." He put a finger to his lips, then said, "Or maybe you didn't tell me because you wanted to be bigger than me." The words hung in the air until Gregory chuckled. "No. How stupid of me. We're best friends. I know you would never treat me so poorly. The correct answer is that you made a mistake, got in over your head, and now you need my help. Isn't that right, Fitzy?"

Ian had no other way to turn. He was in high school all over again. He wanted to pilot his own ship, but Gregory Worthington owned the fleet.

"Yes, Gregory. That's exactly what happened." He tried to match his new partner's gaze. "Tell me what we're going to do."

Gregory grinned his magnanimous grin. "I thought you'd never ask!"

CHAPTER 44

MATTHEW WILCOX

There was no way he was going to just watch and listen. That was boring. And he'd already spent a cold and boring evening watching Worthington's compound. By the time the sun rose, Wilcox had his mind set.

It didn't take him long to make preparations. He'd brought only the essentials. And based on the conversation he'd eavesdropped in on, it looked like Fitzy and Gregory were about to make their move.

For the briefest moment, Wilcox thought about killing them both. Making it quick. But what fun was that? No fun, that's how much fun.

The snow provided perfect cover, and by the time the cavalry spun their wheels up the hastily cleared driveway, Wilcox was ready. All he had to do now was wait a little longer.

CHAPTER 45

GREGORY WORTHINGTON

"Special Agent Leo Mercer, meet Ian Fitzgerald."

The former college basketball center offered his oversized hand.

"Thank you for coming," Ian said. Worthington noticed how the agent's hand enveloped his friend's hand and how Ian cringed at the touch.

"It's my pleasure, though my wife wasn't happy about wrapping all the gifts on her own."

"We'll make it worth your while. I promise," Worthington said. "Can I offer you anything? Coffee? Something stronger?"

"I filled up on the way over. How about you tell me what you couldn't tell me over the phone?"

Leo Mercer was introduced to Worthington at a fundraising event for wounded FBI veterans. At first he'd thought Mercer to be simple athletic brawn. Over dessert, and top-shelf bourbon, he found Mercer wanted to make a name for himself at the Bureau. Not that he'd said it out loud, but

Worthington noted the way the former Purdue standout kept glancing at the FBI director with disapproval, especially when his boss's laugh boomed through the din of flowing cocktails. He was a Boy Scout in many respects. But some digging revealed cases where Mercer was investigated for excessive use of force. He was a titan trying to be a man in an organization infested with politics. Worthington figured it was best to keep to the man's true nature.

"I mentioned a threat. A dangerous threat," Worthington explained. "We believe the man responsible not only has ties to a junior reporter at *The Continental Tribune,* but may try to stymie Ian's efforts in his work."

"Fitzgerald & Muse," Mercer said. "Experts in source acquisition." He recited the words like he was reading out of an encyclopedia.

"That's correct. Ian's firm works for some of the most influential news outlets in the world. You can imagine what a collapse of his services might mean."

Mercer nodded slowly. "Do you have any idea who this man is?"

"No. But if you find Logan Whitaker, we believe you'll find your man."

"Do you know the whereabouts of Mr. Whitaker?"

"It just so happens that he's at Fitzgerald & Muse's offices now."

Worthington would not suggest a course of action. He knew the towering American patriot standing before him would come up with his own plan, a plan that no doubt involved pain and suffering for anyone who got in his way.

"Maybe I will take a coffee," Mercer said. "Could be a long day." He cracked his neck from side to side.

"Anything you need," Worthington said. "Ian, can you think of anything else Special Agent Mercer might need to know?"

Ian looked like he was going to crack. The idiot didn't like pills. Didn't even take a multivitamin. What the man needed was a Xanax to calm him down and then a specially formulated pill to keep him going.

"Um, no. I can't think of anything. Just... please find this guy. I'm afraid of what he'll do next."

The jittery jello of flesh actually elicited a response from Mercer. "Don't worry, Mr. Fitzgerald. I won't sleep until—"

A thundering *boom, boom, boom* shook the house, like a giant knocking at the front door.

Mercer pulled his pistol from its holster. "Stay here, Mr. Worthington."

Mercer, gun at the ready, crept toward the sound.

Boom, boom, boom, came the sound again.

"What is that?" Ian whispered.

"Don't piss your pants, Fitzy. Stay here."

Worthington moved to exit, but Ian grabbed his sleeve.

"He told us to stay here," Ian said.

Worthington slapped his friend's hand away. "This is my home. I refuse to be afraid."

But he was afraid. He shouldn't have been. Well-armed guards manned the perimeter. There was even a quick reaction team on call.

I am not afraid, he told himself.

As he slipped from the living room to the hall, *Boom, Boom, Boom* shook his nerves again.

Where were the guards?

By the time he reached the front door, Mercer was peeking through a crack in the curtains.

"Who's out there?" Worthington asked, realizing that he should've come armed as well.

"Mr. Worthington, please go back to—"

"This is my home," Worthington said, more to prop up his guts than to position his power.

"What... " Mercer was squinting, trying to see through the

snowfall. He pulled his phone from his pocket and pressed the screen. "You have my location. I need a team here now." The phone went back in his pocket and Mercer moved from the window to the door. "Lock the door as soon as I'm through. We have a team on the way."

"A team for what?!"

Mercer didn't answer. He took a deep breath, turned the doorknob, and rushed out. Worthington scrambled over to do as the FBI agent instructed, but when he didn't hear gunshots or screaming, he got curious.

Instead of locking the door, he opened it. Snow blew inside, and Worthington's eyes watered as he tried to see what Mercer was doing. The taller man was standing twenty feet away, looking down at something in the snow. Worthington couldn't make out what it was. There was something familiar about the outline.

Ignoring the cold, Gregory Worthington stepped out his front door and walked towards whatever had the FBI agent's rapt attention. Mercer didn't turn as he approached. It wasn't until Worthington was five feet from the scene that things began to make sense.

There was a tremendous splash of red on the ground and four dark forms. The guards! Worthington took another three steps and slipped forward on his designer leather flips flops. Mercer's arm shot out and held him in place.

"You shouldn't be out here," Mercer said.

Worthington's retort stuck in his throat as he looked down and finally comprehended what was lying in the front courtyard of his beautiful home. Four black-clad guards lay twisted in a macabre jest, their bodies contorted to spell Y.M.C.A.

"You have my attention," he heard Mercer say as he looked all around, though visibility was down to a few feet at best.

Worthington was about to ask the special agent if they

should go inside, when he thought he heard laughing coming from somewhere in the deep white snow towards the woods and the river.

CHAPTER 46

DANIEL BRIGGS

"I've identified almost a dozen others. Little or no social media activity. I'm sure if I had better resources, we'd find that some of them actually had accounts before," Logan said.

"Good. Keep working," Daniel said, not looking up from where he was making stacks of files on the ground and taking notes on two yellow legal pads. "Wait. Are there any commonalities? Anything you think links the sources?"

Logan shook his head. "Maybe if we had Fitzgerald's files. But these are Muse's, mostly background and research he did before recruiting them."

"I'm working on Fitzgerald's database. I've got a friend who's good at that sort of thing," Daniel said. Neil Patel had gladly dropped Christmas preparations at SSI's main headquarters, Camp Spartan, to put his hacker skills to good use. So far, there was nothing.

Logan looked over his shoulder to make sure Marty Muse was far enough away that he couldn't hear. "Do you think we'll find anything?"

"Possibly."

"That's not very encouraging."

"Sometimes an investigation gets boring before it gets exciting," Daniel said.

"So you *do* have a hunch."

"I have all kinds of hunches, Logan. I've just learned from painful experience that not all my hunches need to be chased. Besides, I think Wilcox is about to make our lives a bit more—"

Marty Muse walked into the room, his face pale and stamped with worry. "I'm not sure I can do this. My nerves. And my wife. What happens if I go to jail? She's never worked. She depends on me."

"If you'd rather go home to be with your wife, we can keep working," Daniel said.

"No. I can't."

Logan stood up. "Mr. Muse, this is important. If we don't get this information now, who knows how Mr. Fitzgerald and his cronies are—"

Muse laughed. "Fitzgerald and his cronies. That sounds like an awful B movie." He ran a hand through his messed hair. "No, gentlemen. It's too late. I can't do it."

"Too late for what?" Logan asked.

As if on cue, a newcomer walked into the room.

"You have exactly thirty seconds to tell me what's going on, Logan," Fiona Graves said, arms crossed over her chest. "Because I just got a very concerning phone call from Gregory Worthington. Please tell me why the man who was about to buy a majority share in *The Continental Tribune* thinks you're a murderer."

CHAPTER 47

LOGAN WHITAKER

The silence stretched.

"Ms. Graves, I can explain," Logan somehow got out of his mouth.

"Fiona, thank you for coming," Muse said, looking like he wanted to hug the woman. "You have to help me. I didn't know anything, I swear. It was all Ian, he's been—"

Fiona held up a hand. "Say nothing. I don't want to know. I'm not here to help you solve the crime. I'm here to shut this down."

"But, Ms. Graves, it's all here!" Logan said, holding up a file. "He's guilty. I can prove it!"

"Are you sure? Have you found a smoking gun? Do you have verifiable video of Ian Fitzgerald killing someone? You know what, don't answer that. This is for the authorities to unravel, not me." She walked over to where Daniel was sitting cross-legged on the floor. "Should I even ask who you are?"

"Just a friend, ma'am."

"At least you've got manners. Let me give you a tip, friend. Leave now. I'll take it from here."

To Logan's surprise and shock, Daniel got up from the ground and said, "Sure. No problem."

"It's good to see that someone understands the gravity of the situation," Graves said.

Logan's eyes followed Daniel, who was walking towards the exit. He didn't look back. Not until he was almost out of sight. Then, when Fiona went to comfort Muse, Daniel turned around, looked straight at Logan, and winked. He put a finger to his lips, then disappeared.

Logan breathed a sigh of relief. When he faced Fiona Graves, he didn't have to fake his calm.

"Ms. Graves."

Fiona didn't stop whispering to Muse.

"Ms. Graves."

Her head swiveled slowly.

"Yes, Logan?"

"I'm right."

"Excuse me?"

"You've always told me to follow my gut. You said that when no one else believed you, you stuck to your guns. Those were your exact words. Now, I'm doing the same thing. Why can't you believe me?"

Her face softened. She turned all the way around to face him. Graves looked tired. Logan wondered what she'd been doing before making the trek to Fitzgerald & Muse's offices.

"What happens if I believe you, Logan?"

"If you believe me, you let me investigate. We write the story and show the world what Fitzgerald's been doing."

Graves reached over and put a hand on Marty Muse's arm. "And what about Marty? Have you thought about him?" She pointed to the filing cabinets. "Have you thought about all the people that will be affected? Have you considered all the stories? They'll question them all. What about the future? Will there be any way to verify that the truth is the truth? Because if you have answers for all those questions, then yes, maybe you know more than me, more than Marty, more than every journalist on the planet. Because all this feels like is a mess; an illegal morass that only threatens to get bigger and bigger the more strings you pull from the rug. Are you ready to do that, Logan? Are you ready to dismantle the industry you fought so hard to be a part of?"

"How can we not?"

Graves nodded. "This won't be the last time you ask that question. I never told you this, but I buried eight stories in my career that I believed with all my heart deserved to be shared with the world."

"Why did you do it?"

She stepped forward and looked him in the eyes. "We're not the judge or the jury, Logan. We're reporters. We report the facts."

"But the facts are being manipulated!" Logan wanted to scream.

Graves shrugged. "Can you name a point in history when people didn't manipulate facts? What have we learned about eyewitness accounts? They're unreliable. Witnesses remember what they want to remember. Or worse. They remember what's planted in their minds by well-intentioned journalists, police, politicians, even friends. The victors write history. I don't like it either. But you must learn to work within the system to accomplish anything.

"It's not fair. The facts are the facts. You said it yourself," Logan said.

"I know. But I promise, you've got a long career ahead of you."

"You think so?"

"I know so. I'm the boss, remember?"

Logan nodded. "Okay. I'll do whatever you need me to do."

Graves patted him on the hand. "I was hoping you'd say that. I know you're not a murderer, Logan, but you need to tell me what you know about the man who is doing the killing. Who is the killer harassing Ian Fitzgerald?"

Logan saw nothing wrong with telling her. "His name is Matthew. I don't know his last name. And if he ever finds out I told you his name, he's going to kill me, too."

CHAPTER 48

MATTHEW WILCOX

He'd heard whispers about Leo Mercer, the FBI agent with an acute case of the fix-its. From what Wilcox pieced together, the guy who missed his chance of going to the NBA now wanted to remake the FBI into what his hero, J. Edgar Hoover, had intended: a staunch legion of agents with baseball bats in their hands and pencils up their butts.

How he'd laughed when he watched Special Agent Mercer take in the artwork Wilcox left on Worthington's front doorstep. The shock was brief. The fiery indignation came quick. And the look on Worthington's face? Priceless.

"The hounds are coming. The hounds are coming," Wilcox chanted as he tramped a path away from the expansive estate. The SUV was just where he'd left it. The nice old lady he'd commandeered it from was still sitting in the back seat, covered in a thick blanket. He'd been careful not to cinch the cuffs too tight. She'd eaten two of the four snack bars he left with her, along with some of the water.

"Doing okay?" Wilcox asked when he opened the door, checked the cuffs, and tucked in the blanket.

"I'm missing bridge club," the lady said.

Wilcox smiled. "You sure you wouldn't rather stick with me? You've got nerves of steel, Theresa."

"No thank you, I would not."

Wilcox closed the door and went to the driver's seat.

"Suit yourself. But you strike me as a woman who's seen her share of excitement. You don't care to take life for another spin?"

Theresa's eyes went cold. "Three tours in Vietnam as a nurse, twice widowed, and a grandson who prefers cats to dogs. No thank you, I'll stick to bridge and bird watching from now on."

Wilcox laughed hard. "Fair enough. Last question before I drop you off in town."

"You're mighty chatty for a young man who kidnapped an old woman and snuck off to do who knows what while you left me here to freeze."

"First, you were plenty warm. Second, I am chatty. Thank you for noticing. Now for my question: you're not afraid of me. Why?"

Theresa grunted, obviously amused. Wilcox liked her very much. Very, very much. "You're crazy. I can see that in your eyes. I've seen my fair share of crazy. But deep down, you're not a mean man. I've seen that too. Young soldiers who get their rocks off torturing animals and each other. It's sick. You're not sick. You're just touched, as my grandmother would say. Now get this car moving. I suspect you're about to make a mess of my day if we don't go soon."

Wilcox put the sturdy little SUV in drive, moved out from under the towering tree and headed the long way towards town.

"I think I love you, Theresa," he said.

"Keep dreaming. And don't run off the road. I paid cash for this car. I hope to have it until they take away my driver's license."

Wilcox laughed again. Yes, this was shaping up to be a marvelous adventure, after all. He only hoped it wouldn't end too soon. He wasn't ready for the punchline yet. There were things to do and people to kill. Many people to kill. He could only hope.

CHAPTER 49

IAN FITZGERALD

"We're all gonna die," Ian said, curled up in a ball on the couch.

Gregory marched over and slapped his friend across the face.

"Snap out of it!"

Ian shrunk further into the cushions.

Gregory grabbed him by the hair and yanked him off the couch, onto the floor, and started kicking him in the stomach. Ian wrapped his arms around his legs and tried to hide from the pounding; from the world.

The kicking stopped. All Ian could hear from inside his cocoon was Gregory's heavy breathing. When he sensed that his abuser had walked away, he chanced a look up. Gregory stood with his arms crossed, staring out the enormous window.

Ian got to one knee. Then the other. He winced when he stood up.

"Look who decided to join us," Gregory said bitterly.

"Shall we go another round to clear your head enough to help me?"

Ian realized that his head had cleared.

"Yes."

"Yes what?"

"Yes, I can help. I'm sorry."

Gregory glared at him.

"This is why you should've come to me sooner. I have experience with this sort of thing."

"You have experience with killing people?" Ian asked.

"No, of course not! I have experience with disaster, having my back against the wall, fighting the fight." Ian doubted it, but he made no move to correct his host. "Mercer is on his way to your office. He'll put Whitaker in shackles, beat the truth out of him, find the lunatic behind the defilement of my property, and we're back in business."

"What about Fiona? I don't think it was a good idea to get her involved."

"Look at who has an opinion again. Tell me, Fitzy, why wouldn't we want Fiona Graves on our side? She has a vested interest in keeping the status quo."

Ian had to be careful. He'd shown his hand before. If he got out of this alive, he needed a measure of standing. Would he forever be second place in Worthington's world?

"She's a journalist, through and through. Fiona eats, sleeps and breathes the truth," Ian said.

"Yes. But she's also a realist. She knows what will happen if news leaks of your dealings. It will not only ruin her company, it will ruin her standing amongst her peers. Besides, I offered to buy her paper. She knows which side she's on."

Ian's eyes went wide. "Buy her paper? We can't do that. Do you know what—"

Gregory pointed to himself. "*I* can do anything I'd like.

You need to stay in the lane you've chosen for yourself, the pitiful place you've created."

There was no use arguing. Gregory was right. He held all the power. Unless...

"You're right," Ian said. "I'm sorry."

Gregory gave him a quick nod. In his mind, he'd put Ian in his place. That was how he'd always been, as long as Ian acted contrite. Ian had become very good at acting contrite.

"Let's move on. I think we should be there when they arrest Whitaker. Mercer won't hold back."

"I thought you trusted him."

"I don't fully trust anyone... except myself."

There was the pompous prickery again. *Good,* Ian thought.

Special Agent Mercer opened the office door and marched inside.

"I'm heading into the city. My people have the place surrounded," he said.

"That was fast. Impressive considering the storm," Gregory said. "Would it be possible for us to tag along? You know, to witness the arrest."

"That's not how we work, Mr. Worthington. I can assure you that—"

"I understand, truly. But Mr. Fitzgerald and I would feel much more comfortable staying with you. For protection. You would have our undying gratitude. And I'm happy to pick up the tab for your team's expenses."

Mercer thought on the request for a long moment, then said, "Very well. But you do what I say when I say it. It's the only way I can keep you safe. Agreed?"

"Agreed. Come on, Fitzy, let's go for a ride."

Ian nodded and followed along, all the while piecing his own plan together. It was a long shot. Now, if he could only find a moment to send a message.

CHAPTER 50

DANIEL BRIGGS

He sensed the tail before he saw them. They were good, but not invisible. The trick was to stay close to where he'd left Logan, but somehow lose the two men following. Not two. It was three. The guy at the corner with the blue umbrella glanced his way a moment too long.

Three on one. Fair odds, Daniel decided.

The Beast's growl tingled Daniel's senses. *Yes, I want it too,* he thought.

He slowed his pace. There were plenty of places to hide. But he didn't want to hide. He needed to make it look like he was just another guy on just another snowy day in the city. Daniel doubted they knew who or what he was. He needed to find out exactly who they were. He hunched over a bit more, playing the cold traveler.

Slipping down a side street, he saw the second man walk by, probably telling his partners where Daniel had gone. The Marine sniper leaned against the brick building, counted to nine, and sat down in the snow.

Ray Spadaro cursed the snow as he responded to the text from his partner. He hadn't seen their target cut down the side street. It was his turn to take the lead. The others knew what to do.

Spadaro, a native of Upstate New York who'd wandered to the city in his early twenties, officially called himself a security specialist. What he was secretly calling himself today was a fool. It was Christmas Eve. His wife was angry because he left. They had company coming; the kids were making a wreck of the house, and she expected him to babysit her should've-been-dead-a-long-time-ago father.

Maybe this was better than being at home. Besides, Special Agent Leo Mercer had offered to pay double their normal overtime rate. It was Christmas, after all. Who the hell worked on the biggest holiday of the year, and who the hell put up with all this snow?

He didn't see the guy at first. Spadaro expected to catch a glimpse of the blonde man at the end of the narrow street. But there he was, sitting against the building, staring at his lap.

"Put your hands where I can see them," Spadaro said, slipping the pistol from his pocket.

The guy didn't move.

"I said, put your hands where I can see them!"

The guy's hands went from his lap to the air, slowly.

"You armed?" Spadaro asked.

"No," the man said.

"You high?"

The guy still hadn't looked at him. He was giving Spadaro the willies.

"No."

"Get on your feet."

The man didn't move.

"I said, get on your feet."

Still no movement. Hands were still in the air.

"Look, pal, it's cold out here. Let's get this over—"

The man's head turned, and he looked at Spadaro. Fire burned bright in the man's eyes.

"F…FBI!" Spadaro said, squatting to a shooting position like he'd been taught. Jeez. The guy's eyes. What the hell was wrong with him? Maybe it's me. What the—

"Who are you?" the man with the burning eyes asked.

"I told you. FBI. Get on your feet!" Spadaro said it loud, hoping his partners could hear. He didn't dare reach for his phone. It was all he could do to hold on to his gun.

"You're not FBI. Who are you really?"

How did the guy know? *Shoot him,* Spadaro's survival mind begged. *Shoot him!*

But how would he explain killing the man? "The guy's eyes looked like they were on fire, so I shot him to make it stop?" If he said that, Mercer would make sure to throw Spadaro in jail, or worse. Mercer had a mean streak that the hired gun did not want to provoke.

"Get on your feet!"

Spadaro looked to the end of the street, hoping for his partner. Nothing. Just blankets of snow. He glanced the other way. Still nothing. No help.

When his eyes shifted back to the man, the guy was getting to his feet. *Thank the Lord!*

"Turn around," Spadaro ordered.

The man didn't move. His arms were still in the air. His eyes were locked on Spadaro, though now they looked curious even with the smoldering fire.

Spadaro decided the guy was on drugs. Spadaro hated drugs. He'd had his fair share of run-ins with cracked-up junkies. They had the strength of ten men and were possessed by the devil. Spadaro thought about home, a cozy fire, his wife cooking spaghetti and preparing his favorite dessert, pumpkin pie.

"I don't want to hurt you," the man said.

Spadaro gripped his pistol hard.

"I'll shoot," he said.

"No you won't."

"Yes I will."

Before Spadaro could react, the man lept forward, grabbing for his gun. Self preservation took over. Special Agent Leo Mercer be damned. He pulled the trigger, bracing for both the impact of the man and the report of his gun. The gun didn't go off.

That was when it clicked in his head. The rookie of rookie mistakes. He'd left the safety on.

The man with the blonde pony tail and blazing eyes yanked the gun from Spadaro's grasp and grabbed him by the front of the jacket.

"Are you really FBI?" the man asked.

Spadaro didn't want to die. He just wanted to go home and never take a call from Mercer ever again. Let him do his own dirty work.

"No! I'm just a guy. Please. I have a family. It's Christmas."

It was all Spadaro could think to say.

"How many of you?"

"Three. Just three here."

"And at the office building?"

"Five I think. But I'm not in charge of them. Please, if you let me go I won't—"

"How much time do we have?" the man asked. The gun was now pressed into Spadaro's belly.

"A couple minutes. I don't know."

"How do you communicate with your team?"

"My phone."

The man pulled Spadaro closer.

"Pull out your phone, slowly. Tell them you lost me. Tell them to go home."

"Okay. Sure. But what about Mercer?" Spadaro spit out before he realized what he'd said.

"Who is Mercer?"

Fuck it. He'd rather give up the agent than take a bullet in the gut and bleed out in the snow.

"Special Agent Leo Mercer. He's the guy in charge."

"He's the one who hired you?"

"Yeah."

"Is he at the office building?" the man asked.

"Not yet. He's on his way."

Spadaro thought he detected humor in the man's flaming eyes.

"Good. Text your team."

Spadaro didn't need to be told again. He pulled out the phone slowly, typed the message:

> Lost the guy. Mercer says we're done. Go home. Merry Christmas.

He held it out for the man to see.

"Perfect. Send it. Then give me your wallet."

"My wallet?"

The pistol pressed in harder.

Spadaro sent the text.

"Sure, sure. Here."

Spadaro handed over his wallet.

"There's a couple hundred in there. Take it."

The man let go of Spadaro's shirt, kept the pistol pressed into his belly, and grabbed the wallet with his left hand. He opened it deftly and flipped to the driver's license.

"Raymond Spadaro. Is that your real name?"

"Yeah."

The man tucked the wallet into Spadaro's shirt.

"I don't want to see you again, Raymond Spadaro of 283 Juniper Street."

The man pulled the pistol away and took a step back.

Spadaro was so relieved that he almost dropped to his knees. "You got it. And keep the pistol." Spadaro backed away, still expecting the man to shoot him at any moment.

"Go," the man said.

Spadaro didn't have to be told again. He spun on his heels and sprinted back the way he'd come.

DANIEL BRIGGS

Daniel inspected the weapon in his hand, ejected the magazine to confirm that it was full. It might come in handy.

He waited five minutes to make sure Spadaro's buddies didn't show. They didn't.

Then, he walked back towards Logan and more hired guns. *A Special Agent of the Federal Bureau of Investigation.* What sort of federal agent would hire private contractors on Christmas Eve instead of calling in more agents? It was time to find out.

CHAPTER 51

SPECIAL AGENT LEO MERCER

He'd arrived at the Worthington compound thinking that maybe this was a bad idea. It was Christmas. The call from Gregory Worthington was for him, not the FBI. Mercer understood what that meant, and he was fine with it.

Still, he assumed it would be an errand for a man with whom Mercer very much wanted to curry support. They saw the world the same way, that an iron fist was the only way to protect their country. Mercer didn't mind running errands if it meant getting deeper in the good graces of a man who had more money than Mercer would see in a hundred lifetimes. The money didn't matter to Mercer. The power did.

The four dead bodies on Worthington's doorstep had come as a shock, although a brief one. Mercer fully expected a sniper's bullet as he stood over the dead. When it didn't come, he knew it was a game. Leo Mercer had always been good at winning games.

All thoughts of Christmas were gone. This was a job for a man of his talents. There was a killer on the loose, and Special Agent Mercer intended to find him today. He couldn't wait to see the look on the director's face when he dumped the dead bastard on the past-his-prime director's desk. Not really, but metaphorically for sure.

"Hold on," Mercer said, taking another tight turn and doing his best to not run off the snow-covered road. He thumped against the curb, but somehow righted the vehicle and kept going. The Fitzgerald guy's face kept going from gray to green. He'd told the man not to puke in his car.

He glanced at the text message on his phone.

Follow team disengaged. Subject gone.

Mercer had sent Spadaro's three-man team to follow the stranger, more as insurance. There was no cause to think that the man was a threat. Probably just a guy Whitaker wrangled into helping with Muse's files. Mercer would deal with Spadaro later. No way he was going to pay the man's fee for failing. The contractor would understand, or Mercer would make him understand.

"Do you think he'll be there?" Worthington asked from the passenger seat.

"Who?" Mercer said.

"The killer."

"Maybe."

"Special Agent Mercer, while I understand you have your hands on the wheel of this vehicle in horrid weather, and you're probably trying to unravel the case as it stands, I would very much like to understand what it is you think we're walking in to."

"You wanted to come," Mercer said.

"Yes." Worthington waited.

Mercer exhaled. "Fine. You wanna know the truth?"

"I do."

"We're dealing with a psychopath. A professional killer

who wants something from you and Mr. Fitzgerald. I think it's time to tell me what that is."

"I'm sorry, I can't."

That meant it was valuable.

"Then I can't tell you what this guy is going to do or how he'll do it."

Take that, Mr. Billionaire, Mercer thought.

"Aren't you concerned with your career?" Worthington said, a little too slyly for Mercer's taste.

"Of course I am. What kind of question is that?"

"Oh, I don't know. I just assumed that you knew that what benefits myself and Mr. Fitzgerald also benefits you."

This was the line Mercer had to balance. On one hand, he believed in integrity and upholding the law. On the other, he believed that justice be served, no matter the cost.

"I won't do anything illegal," Mercer said.

"And I would never ask you to! Maybe the better question would be, how much do you want to know?"

The magic question. The longer Mercer was with the Bureau, the farther he strayed from what was accepted. He often thought about what Director Hoover would've done. Hoover revolutionized law enforcement. Mercer wanted to bring the Bureau back to its glory and far away from its recent failures. That meant a hard hand and a cunning mind.

"When the time comes, I might ask for the truth. For now, let me focus on finding the killer. Agreed?"

Worthington grinned. "Agreed. You know, Leo, your list of supporters continues to grow. Why, just the other day I spoke with—"

Mercer listened as he navigated his way through the city, imagining the picture Gregory Worthington was painting inside his head. It was becoming so clear he could almost touch it. This might just turn out to the be his best Christmas present ever. For the first time that day, Mercer smiled.

CHAPTER 52

MARTY MUSE

Marty wasn't sure he had any nerves left. It was getting late. His wife kept texting. He told her there was an important project. At first, she believed him. As the hours ticked by, he could sense that her trust in him was fading. Marty Muse was a good husband. He never missed dinner when he was in town. And he rarely left the city anymore. He loved his life. He loved his wife even more today.

What have I done? he asked himself for the hundredth time that day.

"Marty, are you okay?" Fiona asked. She was the one babysitting Logan Whitaker. Thank God for that.

"I need to go."

"Marty, we've discussed this. I need you here. You have to confront Ian."

Marty didn't want to confront anyone. He wanted to run home and pretend this mess never happened.

"I don't think I have the strength," he said, glancing over at Whitaker. "And what about him?"

"What are you worried about?" Fiona asked.

"Trouble."

Fiona chuckled. "Didn't you know that was the business we signed up for, Marty? You've just been away from it for too long. I promise everything's going to be okay."

"You sure?"

"I'm sure." Fiona's phone dinged with a new text. She looked at the screen. "They're here."

Marty's stomach wrenched in knots.

"I can't do it. You do it for me."

"You'll be fine. Take a deep breath. It'll be over before you know it."

Fiona patted him on the arm.

Three men walked into the room. A towering, official-looking gentleman in a trench coat. Ian Fitzgerald, looking about as awful as Marty felt. And Gregory Worthington. Marty had met the billionaire once, and he'd felt a foot tall compared to Worthington's high-priced friends.

"You must be Ms. Graves," the giant said.

"And you are?"

"Special Agent Leo Mercer, ma'am. Is that Whitaker?"

Marty saw Logan's face go blank.

"Yes, that's him," Ian hissed. "Pain in my—"

"Now, now, Fitzy," Worthington said. "No need to be crass. Let Agent Mercer do his job. Marty, it's a pleasure to see you again."

Marty tried to bob his head but couldn't.

The FBI agent stomped over to Logan and glared down at him. "What's your name?"

Logan sat up straighter. "Logan Whitaker, I'm a reporter with—"

Mercer's backhand almost knocked Logan out of the chair.

"There's no need for that!" Fiona said.

Mercer wasn't through. He grabbed Logan by the hair and yanked him to his feet. He leaned over to whisper something in the younger man's ear. Marty couldn't hear what he said, but Logan's face went pale.

"You, come here," Mercer said, pointing. It took Marty a long moment to realize he was the one being beckoned.

"What? I… there's nothing—"

"Come here," Mercer growled.

Marty somehow moved his feet in a sort of shuffle. He didn't want to get too close, as if the proximity of whatever act this was might slough onto him.

"I said, come here." Mercer pointed to a spot next to him. He was still holding Logan by the hair.

Marty complied, shuffling closer, his heartbeat thudding in his ears.

"Listen up, Mr. Whitaker. You've got one chance to get this right. Understand me?"

Logan's wide eyes glanced at Marty, his fear radiating.

"Yes," Logan said.

"Are you armed, Mr. Whitaker?"

"What? No!"

"And you, Mr. Muse. Would you like to press formal charges against this man?"

Formal charges? What was Mercer talking about? This was about Ian, wasn't it?

"I don't know," Marty said. His hands were shaking. He thought he might pass out.

Mercer ignored him. "How does that make you feel, Mr. Whitaker? Does it make you angry that Mr. Muse wants to press charges?"

"That's not what he—"

Mercer yanked Logan's hair hard.

"It's a yes or no question, Mr. Whitaker."

Then Special Agent Mercer did something strange. He let go of Logan's hair and grabbed his hand instead. Marty thought the young man was about to be put in handcuffs. Mercer guided Logan's hand to the pistol on his own belt.

"You'd like to grab that, wouldn't you?" Mercer asked, leering.

Logan shook his head, petrified.

Mercer used his free hand to pull the pistol from its holster and then pressed it to Logan's hand.

"How's that feel? Think you could do it?"

Logan tried to pull away. Marty took a step back.

"Don't move," Mercer growled, throwing a steel glare at Marty.

"Do you think this is necessary?" Marty said. Something about the situation gave him courage. "I want to talk to your superior."

The request elicited a grin from Mercer. The gun was still pressed into Logan's hand. "Put your finger on the trigger."

Logan yanked backwards, but Mercer held him in place. He must have hit a pressure point because Logan relented and almost went to his knees.

"I said, put your finger on the trigger."

Marty couldn't calculate what was happening. The gun. Logan. Mercer.

No. He's going to make Logan shoot himself.

Courage sprang up again and Marty went forward instead of back. He reached for the gun, thinking to point the weapon anywhere else. The barrel did move, but not in the direction he intended. When the gun went off, Marty and Logan both jumped at the same time. A second later, Marty felt an awesome pain in his midsection. Had he run into the desk? Or maybe Mercer had elbowed him?

The gun went off two more times, and Marty understood. Stumbling back, he looked down at his shirt that his wife has pressed that morning. She never took his clothes to the cleaners. She insisted. Three blossoms of red spread over the stark white.

He looked up at Logan. The younger man's eyes were wide with shock.

I should feel something, shouldn't I? Marty thought.

He turned to face his partner. Ian stared, mouth half open, as Marty crumpled to the floor, eyes locked on the man whose actions had caused it all. But all Marty could think as his vision faded to nothing was, *I'm going to be late for dinner*.

CHAPTER 53

MATTHEW WILCOX

He'd just jumped from the adjoining roof when he heard the gunshots.

"Sounds like they're getting the party started without me," Wilcox said, brushing the loose snow from his body.

He'd seen Mercer's security detail at each entry point of the building. Not that he'd planned on taking the front door, but it'd taken a little time to find another way in.

His phone buzzed. It was Daniel.

"Mr. Wong's house of fun," Wilcox answered.

"Was that you?"

"You mean the guy who jumped from one building to another like Spiderman?"

"No. The gunshots."

"Nope. Wasn't me. Where are you?"

"Around the corner," Daniel said.

"Excellent! I thought I was late to the party. Meet you there?"

"Matthew, don't—"

Wilcox ended the call. There was no time to wait.

"Time to save the day," he said, rushing over to the rooftop door and getting to work on the lock.

DANIEL BRIGGS

He didn't call back. He knew Wilcox well. This was still a game to the assassin. Only there were innocent lives at stake. Logan's being one of them.

Daniel picked up his pace until he saw Mercer's guy standing next to the side entrance. He slowed to a walk. There was no time to find another way in. He walked straight at the man, and when the man's hand came up to stop Daniel, the gun he'd taken from Spadaro shot out, pointed at the man's face.

"On the ground," Daniel said.

The man's hands came up.

"I'm FBI," he said.

"No, you're not."

The fake agent decided to be brave and reached for his gun. Daniel moved fast, closing the gap and side swiping the man in the side of the head with the butt of the pistol. The guy went down in a heap and Daniel stripped him of his gun and his phone. Then, not finding handcuffs on the man, he pulled the shoelaces from the man's boots and hogtied the man as best he could. There wasn't time for better.

Fortunately, the door was unlocked. Daniel crept inside, hoping he wouldn't be too late.

MATTHEW WILCOX

He cleared as he went, knowing that Daniel would try to beat him to the scene. What scene? Wilcox could only guess. He hoped Logan wasn't dead. Not because he'd cry at the kid's funeral, but because that would take some of the fun out of what he had to do next. Wilcox had a plan, albeit a fluid one. He loved manipulating stuck-up bastards who thought too much of themselves. FBI agents were at the top of his list. They'd been after him for years.

The building wasn't huge. The halls were empty thanks to the holiday. Some kind soul had seen fit to put signs up directing wayward visitors to whichever company they needed. Fitzgerald & Muse was easy to find.

The closer he got, the more he could hear. Someone was screaming. He picked up the pace. Wilcox could almost feel Daniel coming up behind him. There was no way he'd come in second.

Screw it, he thought, sprinting down the hall without regard for the nooks and crannies where Mercer's goons might be hiding. No boogymen popped out.

Wilcox made it to Fitzgerald & Muse just as the screaming stopped. He peeked inside and saw everyone looking down. He couldn't see what they were looking at. It didn't matter. He slipped inside before anyone knew he was there. And oh, did he have a lovely sight picture of Special Agent Leo Mercer's head.

CHAPTER 54

IAN FITZGERALD

Marty is dead…

Marty is dead!

He screamed until he was hoarse.

He remembered meeting Marty for the first time. The shy scrawny New Yorker had shown him around the office, said if he needed anything, anything at all, that he was happy to help. Ian understood Marty didn't have any friends. They'd become an unlikely pair. Marty helped him pitch his first story. Marty proofed it, took off the crusty edges, and gave him a nudge when Ian was too nervous to walk into the managing editor's office.

Marty.

How had it come to this?

He tore his gaze from Marty, possibly his most loyal friend in the world, and glared at Special Agent Mercer.

"You," he said, his voice rough and strained.

"Get a handle on your friend," Mercer said, directing the order at Gregory.

"Have a seat, Fitzy," Gregory said.

"No."

Mercer replaced the pistol in its holster, his other hand clutching the back of Logan Whitaker's shirt. The young man looked like he was about to pass out.

"Sit down," Mercer said.

"No," Ian replied.

The huge FBI agent threw Whitaker to the ground. "Stay there." Then, he marched across the room, straight at Ian. "I said sit—"

Ian looked down at Whitaker. Why? He didn't know. There was a flicker of something in the young man's eyes. Recognition? Ian realized Whitaker had glanced toward the door behind Ian and Gregory. A look of satisfaction formed on Whitaker's face, and Ian looked up at Mercer, who wasn't five feet away, when three rapid shots exploded from behind Ian, and three dots marked Mercer's forehead. Because of the angle, he didn't see the carnage behind. He saw the splatter of brain and blood when Mercer fell, very much dead.

He didn't see Gregory grab Fiona and run towards the back exit. He didn't see Logan Whitaker stand up and walk past him. Ian could only stare at the seeping lifeblood of the man who'd killed Marty.

Marty.

Marty is dead.

CHAPTER 55

DANIEL BRIGGS

Daniel ran into the office moments later. There were two bodies on the ground, and Logan was standing with Wilcox.

"Just like the FBI to send an amateur to do their dirty work," Wilcox said. He looked up when Daniel entered. "Oh, hey! Look who came in second. I told you I'd get here first. Lucky, too. I saved the day!"

"Who is that?" Daniel pointed at the official-looking man with the back of his head blown off.

"Oh, that's Special Agent Leo Mercer of the Federal Bureau of Investigation. Real peach of a guy. Isn't that right, Logan?"

"It is."

"You killed an FBI agent?" Daniel asked, his blood rising. The Beast readying.

"He shot Mr. Muse," Logan said. "I don't think he was a good guy."

Logan looked shaken.

"Tell me what happened."

Logan told him quickly, including Gregory Worthington pulling Fiona Graves away.

"What about him?" Daniel asked. Ian Fitzgerald was down on his knees, cradling Marty Muse's head.

"I don't know," Logan said.

"Let me shoot him too," Wilcox said, cheerily.

"No more shooting," Daniel said. "Why didn't you stop the others?"

"I thought you'd catch them. I was busy with big boy Mercer. Did you see that grouping? I should take a picture for posterity."

"Logan, listen carefully. There are men outside who by now know that something happened. They're pretending to be FBI agents, but they're not. You have a decision to make. Come with us, or go to the police. It's your choice."

"I think you should go to the cops," Wilcox said. "After shooting Muse, I'm not sure your fragile constitution can take any more of this."

"No, I'm coming with you," Logan said.

"You're sure?" Daniel asked.

Logan nodded. "What do we do with him?" They all looked at Ian Fitzgerald, now a broken man.

"As much as I'd like to take him, I don't think we have the time," Daniel said.

"That's the smartest thing I've heard you say," Wilcox said. "Now let's get the hell out of here before the real FBI shows up. You don't want to know how many speeding tickets they have on me!"

Wilcox led the way. As Daniel ran by the partners Fitzgerald & Muse, he said a silent prayer for both men. It was the best he could do at that moment.

CHAPTER 56

IAN FITZGERALD

He'd heard them say something about fake cops. Or was it FBI agents? Ian couldn't remember. His focus was on Marty. Poor, innocent Marty.

"I'm sorry," Ian said. He was the only living man left in the room. There was a profundity to the realization. Everything they'd built. Everything they'd been through. And for what? Bloodshed and ruin? All to be as good as or better than the great Gregory Worthington?

I let my pride get the best of me.

"I'm so sorry," Ian sobbed, kissing Marty on the forehead and then laying his friend's head down on the carpet.

He stood, meaning to face the men who were coming. Mercer's men. Wicked men. Just like him. Men willing to do unspeakable things.

What have I become?

It wasn't supposed to be like this.

What would my father say?

The buffeting snow caught his attention. He walked to the window and looked outside. He couldn't even see the street.

Fresh air. I need fresh air.

Sometimes, when he wanted to be alone, he went to the roof through a ladder well that the building's service manager used to access each floor without having to use the elevators or the stairs. There were wires and access hatches all throughout the old building.

Ian went through the small kitchen, into the back closet, stood up on the folding stool, and climbed up into the nook that led to the ladder.

Up. He climbed up instead of down.

He was out of breath when he pushed the hatch open. Snow cascaded down, and he had to push hard to move the extra weight on the heavy door.

The fresh, cold air was intoxicating.

Ian Fitzgerald climbed out onto the roof and looked all around. He could just make out the skyscraper tops of the city. He'd loved coming to the big city. It'd presented him with so many opportunities. And so many temptations.

Walking to the edge, he remembered coming up to the roof with Marty when they'd first signed their lease. Ian brought an expensive bottle of bourbon, and Marty carried a cheap jug of wine. They talked and dreamed. Their world was open to possibility. They got drunk on the future.

"I'm sorry, Marty," Ian said.

He remembered the chess piece he'd put into play before leaving Gregory's. A piece in motion.

He didn't care anymore. Not a thing.

Ian Fitzgerald brushed off the concrete railing, stepped up, and stepped off into blank space. City workers would find his body eight stories below, the day after Christmas, when the snowstorm passed, and they could finally shovel off the sidewalks.

CHAPTER 57

GREGORY WORTHINGTON

"Pick us up at the pizza place. No, I don't know the address. Look it up!"

Gregory ended the call and looked up and down the street for the tenth time.

"Why are we running?" Fiona asked, shivering. Neither had a coat.

"Did you see what happened back there? That madman was going to kill us!" He fidgeted with his phone. If only his helicopter could come get them. Damn weather.

"I saw the shots. If he wanted to kill us, we'd be dead," Fiona said.

"You don't know that." He saw the SUV. "There he is. Come on."

"Gregory, wait. Do you think it's smart to leave?"

"Are you crazy? Of course it's smart to leave. No more playing with two-bit characters like Mercer. I'm calling the Director of the FBI, the CIA, maybe even the president. Now move, I don't want that lunatic to find us."

They pushed through the snow-covered sidewalk and the driver opened the rear door for them.

"Get us the hell out of here," Gregory said, reaching for the hidden mini bar and pulling out a bottle of vodka. He unscrewed the top and let the liquid pour down his throat. The warmth spread to his gut, and he breathed a sigh of relief. He was scared, freezing, and in no mood to talk.

Why weren't they moving? Fiona was talking to the driver.

"What are you doing?" Gregory asked. He wished the SUV was armored. He'd buy one for Christmas.

"There's something you have to see," Fiona said. "Take us to that address," she told the driver.

"No! Get us out of the damned city!" Gregory screamed.

The driver looked back and forth between the two.

"Gregory, this will fix everything. I promise."

That's when he saw it. The look in her eyes. She had been scared before. But not now. The brazen confidence shone on her face.

Think, Gregory.

"You were part of this," Gregory said, coming to understand.

"Not in the way you think," Fiona said.

He pushed the button to roll up the divider between them and the driver. Before it hit the top, he said, "Go to her address."

The SUV rolled forward and Gregory gave Fiona his full attention. The combination of liquid calm and recognition pushed his curiosity.

"I had nothing to do with what happened back there," Fiona explained.

"Okay."

"Ian and I had a plan. You know what a mess our industry is in. We needed to take it back."

"How?"

"By controlling the narrative."

CHAPTER 58

GREGORY WORTHINGTON

He was impressed. Gregory didn't know Fiona well. That was his mistake. He'd assumed Fitzy was behind it all. He'd paired Fitzy's past with the present. In Gregory's head, his old friend wasn't capable of master deception. He was only half right. As he listened to Fiona explain what they'd done and what was in the works, Gregory Worthington saw she was the brains, and his respect for her grew as the snow-filled blocks went by.

When she finished explaining, Gregory asked, "Why are you telling me this now?"

"I think Ian is finished. He was wrecked before Marty got shot. He's done for now. It's up to us to pick up the pieces and move on."

"You don't strike me as a power broker, Fiona. Everything you've told me makes sense, but you still haven't told me what you want, personally."

She nodded and took a moment to gather her thoughts.

"I've wanted to be a journalist since I was three. My father read *The Washington Post* and *The Wall Street Journal* every morning before work. Front to back. He taught me how to read with the funny pages, back when they were funny. By the time I was in high school, I read *The Journal* while he read *The Post*. Then we'd switch. I loved hearing about war-torn lands and secret investigations. I started a high school paper and was the best reporter on my college staff. I loved finding stories and digging out the truth. I've been all over the world. Warlords and gangsters have shot at me. I've been kidnapped. I've come face-to-face with the worst people on the planet. But I did it because I believed the world had the right to know what was going on in their backyards. I won awards. My peers patted me on the back.

"Then came The Internet. At first, it was great. Things moved fast and the pace of play went at warp speed. I thrived. But the old papers couldn't keep up. News got consolidated. Award-winning writers and on-air reporters got fired. There's always been a shock factor to what we do, the power of the headline and all that; but the push for more eyeballs meant going outrageous. It was all about clicks and ad dollars. I got fired three times. I spent all my savings trying to drum up stories and pitch them to media outlets. They didn't want the truth. They wanted sensationalism. They wanted simple messages that looked good in a two second social media post. They said give the readers what they want, stupid copy that's easy to read.

"I tried to play their game. I tried so hard I almost quit. Then Ian came to me. He said someone in Washington wanted to pay him a lot of money to help craft a series of stories with legit sources around a gray area in legislation. He said he needed my help. I told him no. He told me how much money. That got my attention. By then, I was smart enough to know what you've known from birth: money makes the world go around. I helped Ian craft the narrative, and the client was happy. The legislation went their way. The next time, the fee doubled. I saw the possibilities.

"When I got the job at *The Continental Tribune,* we'd worked out a system. Ian courted the clients, Marty found the sources, and I built the stories. We used all the rules dictated by proper journalism. If anyone peeked under the hood, they'd see that the stories were tight. Shareholders at *The Tribune* were happy because we got the juiciest stories first. Ad dollars 10x'ed overnight. We went from just making a profit to dreaming about expansion. That's where you come in."

Gregory couldn't help but smile. "Do tell." He was ready to marry this woman.

"Our board members still think we're in the traditional media game. We're not. It's a new world and we need to think faster, farther. We need an ownership team with balls and a board with vision. We need you and your money, Gregory."

He laughed and took another swig of vodka. "You have a much better way of telling a story than old Fitzy. It sounds like you really mean it."

"I do. I know my place, and that place is making news."

"Fitzy wanted my place."

"I know."

"And you're telling me you don't?"

Fiona grinned. "How about you handle the money, the high-level introductions, and I handle the rest?"

Gregory stuck out his hand and said, "Give me a pen and show me where to sign." Then he remembered. "But you said you have a surprise. What might that be?"

"You'll have to wait until we get there. I promise you'll like it. It might've been Ian's last gift."

CHAPTER 59

DANIEL BRIGGS

"Maybe they went back to *The Continental Tribune,*" Logan said.

"Doubt it," Wilcox said, leading the way with hands stuffed in his pockets. "I've got someone working on it."

"Who?"

"I got a guy. That's all you need to know."

Logan shook his head. The kid was dealing with things well, including Wilcox's answers. "What about Worthington's place?"

"Nah. That place is a bloodbath," Wilcox said.

"What?"

"Never mind. Come on. It's almost dark. Let's get some coffee and donuts. Hopefully, the cops haven't eaten them all."

They found a place that was open. A kind Egyptian man owned the place. He said they could stay in the cramped store as long as he didn't get a rush of customers. He laughed at his own joke, pointing to the empty streets.

There were three tables in the place. Daniel picked the one in the corner and sat down to eat his donuts and drink his coffee.

"Tell me how you like it," the owner said, meaning the coffee. "My wife gets the beans from a cousin in Eritrea."

Wilcox wolfed three pink iced donuts down before Daniel finished one.

"What?" Wilcox said, in response to Logan's incredulous look. "Killing makes me hungry."

"I'd say so." Logan took a bite of his glazed donut and looked towards the door. "Daniel, do you think we'll find them?"

"We will," Daniel said.

"And then what?"

Wilcox made a gun with his right hand and said, "Pew, pew."

"We can't kill everyone," Logan said. "And Ms. Graves is one of the good guys."

"Yes, we can kill everyone," Wilcox said. "I just need to make sure I have enough ammunition. Think there are any armories around here?"

"Don't listen to him," Daniel said.

"Don't worry. I know that much by now," Logan said, stuffing the rest of his donut in his mouth.

"There you go. Maybe we can find you a sense of humor!" Wilcox grinned. "Now, once the storm is over, we have—" Logan pulled out his phone. Wilcox scowled. "You know how rude that is. I was about to regale you with my prognostication for the coming excursion."

"It's my mom," Logan said.

"How sweet."

"Take the call, Logan," Daniel said, giving Wilcox a look.

Logan pressed the Talk button. "Hey, mom. Merry Christmas Eve!"

Daniel couldn't hear what Mrs. Whitaker said. Logan's face scrunched in confusion, then went white.

"Mom, are you... Mom?"

Logan looked at his phone.

"What happened?" Daniel asked.

"She probably put too much yule in the yuletide," Wilcox said, snatching the last donut off of Logan's plate.

"Logan, what did she say?" Daniel asked.

Logan stared blankly. "They have her."

Daniel sat up straight. "Who has her?"

"He wants to talk to me. He says she'll be safe as long as I listen and do what he says."

"Who?"

"Gregory Worthington."

"I knew it!" Wilcox said, slapping the table and getting a look from the shop owner.

"He's texting me the address. He said you should come too." Logan looked at Wilcox.

"Well, that's stupid," Wilcox said. "Doesn't he know I'm going to kill him? I gave him a warning." *What warning?* Daniel thought. What had Wilcox been up to? "Stupid billionaire didn't listen. You only get one shot with me. Am I right?"

"Did he say anything about me?" Daniel asked.

"No." Logan's phone buzzed, and he set it on the table. "That's the address."

Daniel pressed the link and the map app showed a building five blocks away.

"Come on," Daniel said, scooping up the phone and getting to his feet.

"Woo hoo!" Wilcox said, jumping up and trying to give them each a high five. "You guys are no fun."

Daniel ignored the assassin.

"Logan, she's going to be okay."

"You can't promise that. Look at what happened before," Logan said, sitting despondent.

"He's right, Danny Boy. You shouldn't make promises your butt can't keep," Wilcox said.

Daniel fixed Wilcox with a gaze that struck the assassin still. "I put his mother's life on you. If you don't do everything you can to save her, you are dead."

Wilcox let out a low whistle. "Now *that* I believe."

CHAPTER 60

LOGAN WHITAKER

He knocked on the door tentatively.

"The door's open," a voice said from inside.

Logan opened the door to the modest apartment. His mother sat in a chair in the middle of the living room, Fiona Graves a few feet away, arms tied behind her, and Gregory Worthington had a gun pointed at Mrs. Whitaker's head.

"You," Worthington said.

"Me?" Matthew asked.

"Strip down. Slowly."

"But there are ladies present."

"Strip down. Now."

"Fine. But I do this under protest. I'm calling my congressman in the morning. I don't care if it is Christmas Day."

"Close the door, Logan. And lock it," Worthington said, keeping a close eye on the assassin who was stripping his clothes off methodically, one piece at a time.

"You're gonna be okay, Mom," Logan said.

His mother was quivering.

He closed the apartment door, praying that Daniel could find a way in. Fiona sat rigid. She looked like she'd been crying.

I did this, Logan thought. *This is my mess. I have to fix it.*

"What do you want, Mr. Worthington?" he asked.

"We'll talk once he's taken off all his clothes and I can see that he's not armed."

"You're a perv, Greggy," Matthew said. He was down to his boxer briefs and socks. "There. That better?"

"Spin around," Worthington said.

Matthew spun around.

"Satisfied?"

"Not yet." Worthington took the gun away from Eve Whitaker's head and pointed it at Matthew. "Move forward."

"No."

"I said, move forward."

"You're nuts."

"Would you rather die naked?"

"Maybe. Let's ask the ladies."

"Enough!" Worthington boomed. "You and your jokes. They're over, and so are you."

Matthew puffed out his chest. Logan saw the various scars on the assassin's body. "I don't think you have the balls."

"Oh, I think I do."

The gunshots made Eve Whitaker crouch down in her chair. Logan looked right and saw that Matthew was on the ground. He'd landed on his pile of clothes. He wasn't moving. Blood was pooling on the ground.

"Finally! One nuisance down," Worthington said. "Now, Mr. Whitaker. What do you say you and I have a man-to-man talk? I'm sure you're ready to put this unhappiness behind you."

CHAPTER 61

DANIEL BRIGGS

There was no ladder. No way in from adjoining apartments. And the lock on the door would take too long to pick. Daniel put his ear against the door and listened. He could just make out voices, but couldn't hear what they were saying.

I have to break it down, he thought.

Daniel backed up as far as he could. Doors were a funny thing. They made it look easy on TV. But this was an older building with real wood doors. Hefty and strong. If there was an additional deadbolt on the other side, it would be tough, but not impossible.

On the count of three. One, two---

Two gunshots boomed from the apartment. He thought he heard something thud on the floor, like a body falling to hardwoods.

There was no time to waste.

The Beast in him howled, and Daniel Briggs ran straight at the locked door.

CHAPTER 62

GREGORY WORTHINGTON

"You're good, kid. I'll give you that. How would you like to lock in employment for, say, the next twenty years? We can handshake the deal right here and now," Gregory said.

"Anything. As long as you promise not to hurt my mom."

Gregory rested a hand on Eve Whitaker's shoulder.

"I promise. But you'll have to make a promise to me."

He checked again to make sure that the man he'd shot wasn't moving. Nothing. Just a body and blood.

"What promise?" Logan Whitaker asked.

"Fiona says you have skills. I want you to promise that you'll follow her lead. Write the stories she wants you to write. She's agreed to mentor you. You're a lucky young man."

He watched Logan look at Fiona, who looked back with pleading eyes. Oh, how that made Gregory want to smile. He liked her very much.

"I promise," Whitaker said.

"Fantastic. Now, to solidify our deal, why don't we catch a ride to my place and—"

The apartment door burst in and a man with a blonde ponytail barreled inside.

"Put the gun down," the newcomer said, very calmly despite just having used considerable strength to get inside. Wildfire blazed in the man's eyes. Gregory found himself complying. He bent down, set the gun on the floor, and put his hands up.

"Okay," Gregory said, standing back up. "Who are you?"

Complications. Always complications.

"Logan, help your mom." The man looked down at the bleeding body. Gregory wasn't sure if it was grief or something else on the blonde man's face.

"You get Ms. Graves," Logan said, walked forward, kicking the gun away, and going to untie his mother.

Gregory stepped to the side, watching as the blonde man bent down to check on the crazy bastard Gregory had shot. When he stood back up, he turned to face where Fiona had been sitting. Only she wasn't sitting anymore. She was standing. And she was holding her own gun. And before the man could bring his own weapon up again, shots split the silence, and Gregory smiled.

CHAPTER 63

DANIEL BRIGGS

There'd been five shots. For the first time since he could remember, Daniel was too slow. By the time he got his gun up, Fiona Graves was lying in her own lifeblood, her eyes fixed on the ceiling.

"Ding dong, the witch is dead," Wilcox said from the ground. He moaned and rolled over. Blood covered his chest. "Think you can handle the rich guy, Snake Eyes?" Wilcox lost consciousness and Daniel locked eyes with Gregory Worthington. The billionaire's smug air was gone, replaced by fear.

"I didn't know…"

Gregory Worthington's last words were drowned out by the shots Logan Whitaker fired into the man's chest. Worthington slipped to the ground, onto his back. His eyes stared at the ceiling, unbelieving. Logan nudged the man with his foot. Worthington's mouth moved soundlessly, then froze forever.

After a quiet moment, Logan went to his mother and said, "Come on, Mom. Let's go home for Christmas."

EPILOGUE

DANIEL BRIGGS

"Merry Christmas, Mom."

Logan picked up his mother and hugged her in front of the fireplace. She giggled and said, "Put me down, Logan." He put her down, and she looked up at him. "You remind me so much of your father."

"Cut it out, Mom. Daniel will think we're like this all the time." Logan gave Daniel a wink.

"From what you've told me of Mr. Briggs, I think he's just fine with me showing my only son a little love." She stretched up and gave him a peck on the cheek.

"She's not wrong, Logan," Daniel said.

It was a simple affair in a fancy penthouse. Eve Whitaker was what Daniel expected: loving and understanding. She'd shaken off the shock of being taken from her home, shipped to New York City blindfolded, and tied to a chair with surprising grace. Daniel saw the deep glow of faith all around her.

They'd made it.

It was Christmas morning, the snow outside was drifting

instead of dumping, and the dead bad guys were being dealt with by Daniel's friends.

"Is anyone hungry?" Daniel asked.

"I'm starved. You think anyone's open?" Logan asked.

The doorbell rang and Daniel said, "Just in time. Special delivery is here."

Daniel rose from the couch and smiled when his friends appeared. Liberty, the beautiful German Shorthaired Pointer, came first, barreling into the room. Eve Whitaker squealed and moved to intercept the dog, who went to her willingly, showering her with licks and full-body snuggling.

Cal Stokes, Willie Trent and Gaucho came in next.

"Santa's here," Cal said, carrying a teetering tower of presents wrapped in shiny red paper.

"And so's the chef," boomed MSgt Trent, hoisting grocery bags into the air.

"And so's the Mexican!" Gaucho hooted, laughing at his own joke and rushing over to Daniel to wrap him in a hug. "I've missed you, Snake Eyes."

"You too, Gaucho. Guys, I want you to meet Logan Whitaker and his mother, Eve."

Everyone shook hands. Then Trent went to the kitchen, Gaucho went to make drinks, and Cal stayed in the living room.

"You've been busy," Cal said, putting an arm around Daniel.

"A bit."

"You look good. Definitely better than the last time."

Daniel chuckled. "I'll bet. You get everything worked out with the Feds?"

"Yep. The Worthington family might not be happy, but the FBI is beside themselves about Mercer. Sounds like he was a thorn in the director's side. It was a quick conversation. You took care of his problem."

"I wish I could take the credit, but it was Matthew."

Cal rolled his eyes. "And where is our intrepid assassin now?"

A squeaking caught everyone's attention as Matthew Wilcox shuffled into the room in a robe and pushing an IV stand on wheels. "I knew you missed me, Cal. Come and give me a squeeze. But not too hard. My wounds are still healing."

Cal did not give Wilcox a hug, though in hindsight, he thought maybe he should have in order to squeeze a little too hard and make some of Wilcox's stitches pop.

"We almost didn't make it in time. The sky cleared as we were waiting. Helo dropped us off in Central Park. That was fun to see New Yorkers gawking, though they probably thought we were somebody important," Cal said. He took the proffered drink from Gaucho. "What shall we toast?"

Once everyone had a drink, and Top was with them, Daniel raised his glass of ginger ale and said, "To family."

For years, he suppressed his emotions to maintain an even keel. His friends would call it Zen. Now, gazing around the room at his adopted family, tears came to his eyes, and he wished Anna was there with him. He loved her more than he'd thought possible. She understood him, the yin and the yang. How many others were there, men and women who looked to him for friendship, without motive, without expectation? There were many, he realized.

"Hey," Daniel said. "I thought Neil was coming."

Cal, Top and Gaucho all shared a look. "He's working on something," Cal said.

Everyone turned when Wilcox clapped his hands together. "I knew it! Another adventure! When do we go? Tonight. Come on. I'm ready!"

Daniel laughed. "You're not going anywhere. And you're bleeding."

Sure enough, there was a splotch of blood on the white bathrobe.

"What, this? Tis but a flesh wound!"

Everyone laughed at that. And Daniel couldn't help but think that it was much better to be on another adventure together, instead of alone. Adrift and broken were two places he never needed to be again.

I hope you enjoyed this story.

If you did, please take a moment to write a review on Amazon. Even the short ones help!

God-Speed

Running

Chosen

ABOUT THE AUTHOR

C. G. Cooper is the USA TODAY and AMAZON BESTSELLING author of the CORPS JUSTICE novels, several spinoffs, and a growing number of standalone novels.

WHY C. G. Cooper MATTERS

Fiction has the power to change lives.

Pay a visit to Cooper Country and you'll understand why. With his unique voice and flair for creating characters you'd love to hang out with, C. G. Cooper imparts every one of his novels with messages that perfectly illuminate what Faulkner called, "the human heart in conflict with itself." In them, characters confront hard truths about life, the necessity of war, the military industrial complex, and why and how good men and women die.

But there are messages within the messages.

There is the power of the individual to triumph over evil against overwhelming odds; the struggle of good people against their inner demons; the discovery of allies in unexpected places. There is brotherhood, family, community, and authenticity. There are struggles with faith. Cooper's heart is on every page, beating hard and fast through action and moments of tenderness alike.

Expect high-octane action, slow-burn thrills, and gut-wrenching drama. Expect the ultimate conflict of the human heart.

This is Cooper Country. Lives will change.

THE LOWDOWN

Drawing on his days as an infantry officer in the United States Marine Corps—a stint that came on the heels of a degree in foreign affairs from UVA—Cooper sifted his experience through his vivid imagination and created *Corps Justice*, the first novel in the beloved Corps Justice series. Thus, a band of characters was born that would go on to enthrall readers across twenty-plus novels.

With over 300 million pages read in Kindle Unlimited and multiple appearances in the Amazon Top 100, C. G. Cooper remains one of the most successful authors on Amazon.

In 2020, he won the prestigious James Webb Award presented by the Marine Corps Heritage Foundation for his novel *Chain of Command*.

In addition to bouncing around the country in search of the

perfect vacation (turns out, it is anywhere with his family), Cooper has called Nashville home ever since his final Marine duty station. When not enjoying the laid-back lifestyle of Music City, he's doing his best to add more novels to the growing list at www.cg-cooper.com.

Cooper loves hearing from readers and responds to every email personally.

To connect with C. G. Cooper, visit
www.cg-cooper.com

Made in United States
Troutdale, OR
02/05/2025

28706201R00159